MW01140035

tautened

a threads novel
book one

adrian page

This is a work of fiction. The characters, incidents, and dialogues are products of the author's imagination and are not to be construed as real. Any resemblance to actual events or persons, living or dead, is entirely coincidental.

Tautened
Copyright © 2016
All rights reserved.
No part of this book may be used or reproduced in any manner whatsoever without written permission, except in the case of brief quotations embodied in critical articles and reviews.

ISBN-13: 9781695374805
ISBN-10: 1537324543

for Anastasia and Sylv
I wouldn't have gotten here without you.

thank you

one

Until that moment, I hadn't realized that heartbreak had an actual, audible sound. It had never crossed my mind that it would. And I certainly didn't think that it would—or could—be so loud. The sound hit me in waves so strong and so deafening that I wasn't sure if it was coming from my heart or hers. It silenced every animal, insect, gust of wind, whisper of trees. It was as if, in that moment, everything was standing still.

"Is there someone else?" I could hear in her voice how hard she was trying not to cry. I hated myself for doing this to her.

I reached for her hand but she pulled away. "No, Zoe, there's no one else." I tried to lift my gaze to meet hers but I couldn't manage it. Looking at her hurt. "I'm sorry."

"You're *sorry*, Anna? *Sorry*?" Zoe sat up, and I found myself starting at the imprint she'd left in the thick, damp grass. "Look at me."

I did. Her blue eyes looked more watery and translucent than usual, and it occurred to me that in our eleven month long relationship, I had never once seen her cry. I tore my gaze from her face, feeling my breath catch in my chest. Her white shirt was damp with dew and mud, clinging to her desperately. Her arms bore pale red lines and curves from laying on the ground.

"Look at me."

"I am." Something inside me shattered.

"I thought we were okay, you know? I thought everything was okay. And then—what— you went to some party Saturday and now you want to break up? Anna, how am I supposed to believe that there isn't somebody else?"

"It has nothing to do with the party, Zoe, Jesus. I just…" I couldn't find the words. Why was I doing this, again? It was all lost inside my chest. The information had taken a wrong turn somewhere. Never made it up to my brain.

"You just what? You just don't love me anymore?" Her voice finally broke, and I turned away. I didn't want to see her cry.

"No."

"No *what*?" Her voice was wet.

"I don't know."

Zoe stood, towering over me. Her shadow blocked the sun from my eyes but I still couldn't bear to look up. "Well that's just great, Anna. Really. Fantastic. Fuck you."

She should have stormed off. She wanted to. I wanted her to. But she didn't. She just stood there, crying and shaking over me. And I just laid there, splitting long strands of grass down the middle and wondering why I couldn't split them evenly. I could feel the tension in her muscles, radiating off of her. I wondered if she wanted to thrash around, cause a scene, hurt me. I wouldn't have blamed her.

Zoe unfolded her arms and let them drop to her sides. I wondered if she was still crying. I didn't dare look.

"Okay. Fine."

And she left.

I didn't look up until I was sure she was a safe distance away, and even then, I didn't look at her. Instead I looked to the opposite direction, towards the stream, and tried not to remember why I brought her here, of all places, to break up with her. At the time, I thought it was a good idea. But I was starting to think that I had needlessly hurt her even more.

The first time we met, we were there. Drunk with a bunch of mutual friends by the stream only a twenty minute walk from my high school and a ten minute walk from campus. I was sixteen and only seemed to have friends my sister's age. Zoe was up that weekend visiting her brother, who used to be friends with my sister, from Connecticut. I remembered thinking that she was so, so beautiful.

I remembered asking my sister about her and her telling me that her brother had mentioned a girlfriend, once, but maybe they had broken up. I felt bad for it, but all hearing the word 'girlfriend' did was give me hope. She wasn't straight. *I stood a chance.*

The first time we kissed we were there, too. Almost a year later when Zoe came up in April to visit her brother during her high school's spring break. I was there again with my sister and her friends, drinking by the stream, and she showed up with her brother and sat down next to me. We started talking—I couldn't tell you what about. God, I was so stupid, but it took me about an hour and a half to realize that she was actually flirting with me.

One by one and two by two, everyone started to head home. But Zoe and I stayed. I knew she was going home the next day and that it'd be at least a year before I saw her again, if she even wanted to visit her brother once she went away to college. So I asked her if I could kiss her. And she said yes.

I walked her back to her brother's dorm that night, even though it was the opposite direction of the lot my car was parked in. When we got there, she asked me what college I was going to next year. I told her that I'd been accepted and was planning to enroll here. She smiled, and told me that she would be, too.

She gave me her number and her Skype, and we talked every night for the next week and a half. And then she asked me to be her girlfriend.

My sister's friends grew up. They got houses and apartments of their own off campus. The stream fell out of use as our go-to location. But Zoe and I always went there. To drink, to kiss, to talk, to eat, even to fight. It became our place. For better or worse.

Some part of me felt like it had to end where it began. I didn't know if that was because I thought it would hurt more or hurt less. Maybe I didn't want either of us to have this place anymore. Maybe I thought it was better to throw the bad in with the good so we could look at our relationship at face value. I didn't want to spend my time thinking about all the good and ignoring the bad. I didn't want her to do that, either.

I knew breaking up with Zoe was the right thing for the both of us, but I still didn't have the words for why. It was a feeling I had for the last month or two, tucked in between my ribs. Something visceral and nonverbal and impossible to translate. I just knew that we weren't right anymore and that it was better to end it now than drag it out. Better to cut the cord than let it suffocate one or both of us.

I rolled over onto my back, staring up at the graying sky, and started to cry.

"So you don't know why you broke up with her?" Cora looked doubtful. "Anna, that doesn't make any *sense*."

I shook my head and swallowed down the knot in my throat. "No, I mean, I know why. I just... don't have the words." I put my hand on my chest, fingers digging into the flesh just below my breast. "It's right here. Or it was. There was this knot or tumor or feeling or *something*. I knew I had to break up with her. And I did. And the feeling is gone."

That wasn't true. It was still there. Just quieter now. It wasn't wedged between my ribs as tightly as before.

"I thought you loved her." My sister's words cut me, even though she was trying to be gentle.

"I do. I did. I don't know." I buried my face in my hands. "Something changed. A while ago. I don't know what, so don't ask me. Just. I didn't want either of us to get hurt any more than we already were. Are."

"So... in order to not hurt Zoe... you broke up with her. Even though you still love her."

I looked up at her, studying her face. She was trying so hard to understand, but there wasn't anything *to* understand, really. Her brow was furrowed and her dark eyes were searching. I thought that, in that moment, she looked a little bit like me. Or I looked like her, since she was older. Of course, the similarities were in disposition and mannerisms only. But even they were analogous enough to cause me to temporarily forget that my sisters and I shared no more DNA than the average strangers.

"I know it doesn't make sense. But it's done. We're both better off. I have to believe that."

"I know you do," Cora assured me. "It'll be okay. If you think it was the right thing to do, then I'm sure it was. You're usually right about these sort of things."

I offered her a weak smile.

"I have to go to the library now to work on a paper. You gonna be okay?" She reached across my bed and put her hand on my knee.

"Yeah, I'm gonna be okay. I am okay." The smile I attempted was stronger this time. If it were anyone but Cora, I'm sure it would've been pretty convincing. But my sister knew me too well.

She smiled back, anyway. She knew it was important for me to pretend right now. "Text me if you need anything."

"Always."

"I love you."

"I know. I love you too."

Zoe called three times and texted me eleven times by the time I finally decided to get out of bed. I hadn't expected this from her; I was always the one hanging on to *her* in our relationship. The more I thought about it, I realized she probably hadn't expected this from me, either. Zoe always needed to be in control, to see everything coming in any direction, to be able to say 'no.'

I'd always assumed that, if we ever did break up, she'd be the one to leave me. I wondered if she felt the same. If that was why she called me three— no, four; my phone started ringing again— times. Because the way we ended was backwards.

I put my phone on silent and stuck it in my sock drawer.

I got dressed methodically, hardly even bothering to make sure that my clothes matched. I needed to get out of this room. I needed to get some food in me. I needed to straighten my head out. I needed. I needed. I needed.

It was Monday morning and everyone was everywhere on campus, but I didn't have class until noon. I wished I had it earlier for the very first time in my life, because I didn't want to sit around for four hours and think about what I'd done.

I loved Zoe. I was such an idiot. I loved her.

But I still didn't want to undo it. Being with her was starting to feel wrong in a way I didn't really have words for. It made my bones ache. Although, they still ached even after I ended it. I just wanted to make things right. I thought that breaking up with her would make things right.

Maybe was being impatient. Maybe things would be right soon. But when? I was never a patient person. I didn't have the stomach for waiting. It made me sick and queasy and exhausted.

It had only been an hour since I broke up with Zoe. I was going to go mad.

I left my dorm in such a hurry that I forgot my ID on my dresser. I realized it halfway down the hallway, but I didn't bother turning back. Someone would let me in the building sooner or later. I could always call my roommate, August, to let me back in. I'd worry about it later. I didn't have the energy.

I didn't know where I was going. I left the building, left the campus, left the street. I wound up in some residential part of town I'd never been to before. Most of the cheap, student-rented houses and apartments were on the other side of the school.

This was where the townies lived. And students tended to avoid townies like the plague.

The houses were trim and neat, lined up evenly in the most sickeningly suburban way. They had square little lawns and neat brown fences and big trees in the back yards. I hated houses like these, but Zoe loved them. She loved the order and the regularity. We used to talk about having a little house like this someday—or, she did—to raise our family in. I remembered thinking how farfetched and unlikely it was, but playing along because I liked the way her voice sounded when she said it.

I wondered if she believed it. That we'd get married and own a house and have 2.5 kids and a dog and a two car garage with a pool in the backyard. Her perfect average dream life. I never believed in it, but maybe she did. Maybe she believed it was a tangible, real thing. A tangible, real thing I took from her this morning.

I wanted to cry again, but I didn't.

two

sophia jane kalvak
March 15

The kiss was, overall, disappointing. He was stupid drunk and so was I, but even through the haze of the booze, I could tell that this wasn't what I wanted. He pulled me back to him, hands firmly pressed against my glass body, until I was practically sitting on his lap. Something inside me tugged away from him, but my actual body didn't budge. I let his rough paws grope my breasts as his tongue snuck into my mouth. I wanted to gag, but I held it back. Instead, I let it go on for as long as I could bear before pushing him away.

"I'm going to go get another beer," I said, standing up. I could feel the room swaying, almost as if we were on a boat. A wave of seasickness swept over me, but I held my ground. The boy sat on the bed, disheveled and confused, but the eager, hungry look didn't leave his eyes. I forced a smile at him before leaving the bedroom for good. With any luck he'd fall asleep there and forget anything had happened... but I wasn't going to count on it.

The party was still very much alive downstairs, to my surprise. It seemed as though we had been up in his bedroom for several lifetimes; surely the guests must have aged and died in that time. But no, the living room and kitchen were full to capacity with the same unfamiliar faces as before. I wished I hadn't let Emma talk me into coming. I knew most of the people here were her friends and that, for the most part, I was safe, but someone hadn't given the uneasy feeling in my stomach that memo.

Or. Maybe I wasn't feeling nervous. Maybe I was feeling...

I bolted for the bathroom, pushing another girl out of the way to get in first. I was drunk enough that I couldn't quite feel the vomit searing my throat, just the heaving of the muscles in my abdomen. When nothing else would come out, I rinsed my mouth out in the sink and left the bathroom. I thought that maybe I should've apologized to the girl I'd pushed, but she wasn't standing outside anymore. It didn't really matter, anyway.

I wanted to go home badly. I wasn't and would never be the party type; I was too uncomfortable in groups and never seemed to be able to talk to anyone. How I'd even ended up in that bedroom with the boy who lived here was a mystery to me. I glanced around the corner into the living room to see if I could find Emma and let her know I was leaving, but she didn't seem to be there. I recognized one or two faces in the crowd, but my roommate was not one of them. She wasn't in the kitchen, either, so I gave up and went outside. I would just call her once I was back in our room. She would understand.

The cold air felt like a hundred thousand tiny needles on the soft skin of my face. It was mid-March, almost spring, but no one gave the New Hampshire weather the memo. The air smelled thin and sharp. I wondered if it was going to snow.

From inside the house I could hear the hazy melody of a song I knew from some movie I'd seen. It wasn't a party song; it was something softer, mellower. Somehow, it managed to bring out the fog in my head. I wasn't so sure about walking back to my dorm anymore and found myself sitting down on the porch steps.

My head was too heavy for my neck, so I propped my elbows on my knees and held it in my hands, fighting through waves of nausea. I could feel knots forming in my throat, accompanied by the tell-tale stinging behind my eyes. I was going to cry on that stranger's porch. It was inevitable, at that point, and the thought of walking home crying didn't seem any more appealing. So I just let it happen, hoping that no one would come outside and see me.

Of course, that would be too easy.

She almost tripped over me trying to get down the stairs. In retrospect, it was definitely too dark for me to be sitting there and not end up being tripped over.

"Oh—shit—I'm sorry—fuck, are you okay, dude?" she asked once she caught herself. I didn't think I would've been able to formulate a coherent response, so I didn't even try. "No, seriously dude, are you alright?" She sat down next to me, her arm brushing mine.

I peeked at her through my fingers and the black curtain of my hair. I'd never seen her before. If I had, I would've remembered, because she was easily the most beautiful girl I had ever seen in my life.

She was short, a little chubby, and had a smattering of dark freckles on her smooth, brown skin, which just a few shades darker than my own. Her hair was a dark, rich brown, curly, and fell almost halfway down her back. She was looking at me with her big, brown eyes, waiting for a response.

"Yeah, I'm great. Don't worry about it." I lifted my head to look at her, careful to keep my wet face hidden behind my hair.

She frowned, her round nose crinkling, and raised an eyebrow. "You are so not okay, dude. Did something happen? How much did you have to drink, do you need me to walk you home?"

"I'm okay, really. Thanks." I cleared my throat and wiped my face on my sleeve, then sat up completely. "See? Fine. Really." I could feel more tears welling behind my eyes and I begged them to stay there until she left.

I wasn't fooling her, apparently. She reached out and brushed my hair from my face where my tears had glued it. I tried to pretend she hadn't touched me. I tried to pretend that being touched made me want to cry even more. I failed. I started crying.

The stranger pulled me into her arms, her embrace surprisingly encompassing for someone so much smaller than me, and clumsily kissed my hair. "Hey, hey, stop that. You're okay. You're okay." I had never felt so simultaneously embarrassed and comforted in my life. How could she make me feel so foolish and so comforted at the same time? I felt like a child in all the best and worst ways. She kissed my hair again.

"I'm sorry, I don't know what's wrong with me." I pulled away from her and stared down at my hands in my lap. "I'm okay, really, you should go back inside. I'm okay to walk home."

"I'm not letting you walk home alone, dude. Besides, I was going to leave soon anyway. Where do you live?" She stood, offering a hand to help me up.

"Parker," I told her, taking her hand and pulling myself up. "Are you sure? You really don't have to. I'm okay." Even as I said it, I could feel myself start to sway. I probably *could* walk home alone, but it'd be difficult. But I still felt so guilty about making this stranger leave with me.

"No, it's fine. Like I said; I was going to leave pretty soon anyway. I'm exhausted." She wrapped her arm around my waist. "C'mon, let's get you home."

I lost most of the walk home. I knew we talked, but I couldn't remember what we'd talked about. I knew she made me laugh, but I couldn't remember why. By the time we got up to my room on the second floor of Parker, my memory was full of holes. It even took me a minute or so to remember who this girl was and why I'd left the party with her.

I had tried to get her to leave me in the lobby because she lived in Somerset Hall, which was on the opposite side of campus, but she insisted on walking me up the stairs to my room. I didn't protest that too much—I wasn't sure how my Jell-O legs would handle the stairs, and I was honestly enjoying her company.

I put my door code in wrong the first two times because my eyes were heavy and couldn't keep the buttons in place. When the red light on the keypad flashed, I felt heat creep up my neck. It wasn't really anything worth being embarrassed about, but I was regardless. I could feel her gaze resting on my hand as I tried the code again.

6-6-5-7-3.

Bzzzzzt. The green light flashed and my door unlocked. I pushed it open and then turned to face her, half inside and half out. "Thank you so much," I told her, taking extra care to push the words through the thickness in my head.

"No problem…" She glanced at the name tags on my door. "Are you Emma or Sophia?"

I felt myself blush again. Idiot. How did I manage to forget to tell her my name? "Sophia. I'm Sophia." My name stuck in the desert of my mouth the second time, trapped between my tongue and the roof. I pretended I didn't hear how awkward it sounded, but it wasn't as easy to forget anymore. The fog in my brain had cleared just enough.

"No problem, Sophia." She smiled at me, dimples appearing on her freckled cheeks. "You get some rest now, dude. Drink lots of water. Take care of yourself." Her voice was softer than it was before. Almost bordering on maternal.

I laughed, but it felt forced. "I will. Thank you." I rested my heavy head against the doorframe, chewing on my lip. I had a weird, fluttering feeling in my stomach. Something like butterflies but more unsettling and strange. A hundred million eyelashes were brushing against the walls of my abdomen.

"Good," she paused, mouth slightly agape as if there was something more she wanted to say. "Well. Hopefully I'll see you around, Soph." I had never been called Soph before, but I liked it.

"Yeah, hopefully."

She waved by bending her fingers to her palm instead of shaking her hand, like a little kid would. And then she turned to leave.

It wasn't until she was about to round the corner at the end of the hall that I realized that I had never asked for *her* name. Or maybe I had and I'd forgotten it.

"Wait! What did you say your name was again?" Better safe than sorry.

She poked her head out from around the corner. "I didn't. It's Annabella." And then she disappeared around the corner again.

"Annabella," I said out loud, testing the weight of it in my mouth. I liked the way it felt on my tongue, the heaviness of the syllables and the vowels. It was musical, almost. A song I'd just learned.

I suddenly came-to and realized that I was still standing in the doorway, looking off down the hall where she'd left. Heat crawled up my neck and onto my face and I quickly shut the door, letting myself sink to the floor behind it.

Annabella, Annabella, Annabella.

The eyelashes in my stomach fluttered, sending a shiver up my spine and into my throat. I grabbed the trash bin nearest to me—Emma's, but I'd worry about that later—and vomited what was left in my stomach into it. When I was finished, my forehead and back were damp with sweat and I had sobered up considerably.

I knew I should've dealt with the trash then and not let my puke sit until morning, but I was too exhausted at that point. I pushed the bin away from me and stood, only swaying due to the weakness of my muscles. My head felt like it was full of hot air as I crossed the room, took a water bottle from the fridge, and climbed into my bed.

My intention was to drink the water *before* I fell asleep, so I wouldn't be so dehydrated when I woke up, but I couldn't stomach it. I wasn't too worried; I'd never been hung over before in my life and didn't plan on starting then.

The eyelashes in my stomach were slowly turning into hairy spiders, eight lashes at a time falling off the whole and scurrying around my insides. I could feel them in my stomach, my lungs, my throat, my mouth. Crawling. Nesting. Settling.

I needed to get my mind off them, somehow, but though I was exhausted, I couldn't seem to fall asleep.

I found myself thinking about sitting on that porch with Annabella, her arms around me, and I grew inexplicably warm. Orange light was pouring out of my eyes, my nose, my ears, and my mouth. From the cracks in my skin and the beds of my nails. My eyes were closed, but I knew this to be true. I could feel it.

Unfortunately, it seemed to do very little to deter the spiders. They crawled around inside me and turned my stomach with their hairy legs. Despite the fact that I was no longer very drunk, and despite the fact that I knew I was not moving at all, I was starting to feel seasick again.

three
annabella morgan avery
March 16

When I woke up the next morning, my ribs were aching. I rolled over stiffly, turning my back to the wall. August was snoring away on the other side of the room, curled up in a ball on top of her blankets. She hadn't gone to the party with me last night, but she was in her underwear with her clothes thrown haphazardly on the bed and the floor. She always seemed to strip down before bed when she was drunk. I wondered where she'd gone last night.

The room felt sticky and claustrophobic. All at once, I felt the most overwhelming need to leave. I didn't know what it was, but ever since I broke up with Zoe, I couldn't stand to be inside. I needed the air. I needed the space. I couldn't stand feeling confined or trapped. It made me sick.

I got dressed quickly, deciding that going for breakfast was probably my best and safest option. Zoe never got breakfast. She never woke up before noon if she didn't have to. And most of our friends were the same. The chances of me running into someone were minimal, and I really needed to eat something. There was a small animal trapped in my stomach, clawing at the walls. I could feel it crashing and kicking at my ribs.

It was hotter outside than I anticipated, but I deserved to sweat in my long sleeved shirt and sweatshirt combo because I had been too stupid to check the weather or even ask my sister what it was like outside. I had assumed that, because it was snowing last night when I walked home, it'd still be chilly today. As if I hadn't lived in New Hampshire for my entire life. I should've known better.

There weren't many people outside, as was to be expected at ten am on a Saturday. Part of me wished I would run into someone I could grab brunch with. Someone to get me out of my own head for a little while. But I knew anyone I'd see would ask me about Zoe, and I still didn't want to get into it. I knew that our friends knew, but I had been avoiding them for the last week. The longer I went without seeing them, the easier and scarier it became.

The dining commons was empty. I counted nine people on the first floor, three at one table, two at another, and the other four sitting alone. I wasn't surprised, but it was still the emptiest I'd ever seen the place. It had a lonely, sad sort of feel to it.

I grabbed a plate and loaded it up with eggs and hash browns and made my way to the far back corner of the commons, stomach gurgling. I managed to pick the exact wrong seat so that the sun streaming through the windows hit me directly in the eyes, but I was too hungry to bother moving. Instead I opted to just look down at my plate.

I was about half way done eating when I heard someone clear their throat. I swallowed down my eggs along with the knot that noise had formed in my throat and looked up, preparing myself to see Zoe.

She was blocking the light just enough that I could see her if I squinted. A wave of relief washed over me when I realized that it *wasn't* Zoe. It was the girl that I had walked home the night before. Sophia.

She looked so uncomfortable, one arm holding a plate of food, the other pressed tightly to her side. She kept looking at me and then looking down and back at me. I wondered why she seemed so nervous.

"Hey, dude, how are you feeling?" I smiled, trying to make her feel less uncomfortable. I didn't know why she'd approached me. She didn't look like she wanted to. We'd talked a lot last night on the way back to Parker, and she seemed friendly enough then, but maybe Drunk Sophia and Sober Sophia were two entirely different people.

"Oh, uh, fine. No hangover," Sophia said. "I just, y'know, wanted to thank you again for helping me last night. I feel like such an idiot." She looked away again. "But like, I really appreciated it. I don't know how I would've made it back in once piece without you." She laughed a little, but I could tell she was embarrassed.

"No, don't worry about it! It's totally fine. I wasn't about to let you go alone and get lost or hurt or worse," I told her. "And I was getting ready to bail anyway. It was nice to have someone to talk to and unwind with before going to bed, y'know?" I assured her. "I mean, it was nice to have someone actually think my jokes were funny. Drunk or not."

Sophia laughed. "I don't remember any of your jokes, but I do remember thinking you were hilarious."

"Good. Because I am. I'm also wildly attractive and smart, too. In case you forgot." She laughed again. "Are you here with anyone—do you wanna sit down?" I offered, gesturing to my empty table. "Plenty of available seats."

"No, I'm alone. You don't mind if I sit with you?"

"Mind? I'm honored to have you sit with me, Soph." I grinned. "So you're really not hung over? At all? How?" I asked, taking another bite of eggs. "Tell me your secrets, oh Wise One."

Sophia laughed again, and somewhere in the back of my mind I thought that I could listen to her laugh all day and not get tired of the sound. But I left the thought back there where it belonged. My head was a mess.

"I don't know, honestly. I've never been hung over. It's just a superpower of mine, I guess."

"Really? Never?"

"Never."

"Dude, you have no idea how jealous I am of you," I laughed. "I get wicked hangovers," I explained. "Like, debilitating ones. I pretty much have to stay in bed all damn day."

"You're not hung over today, though?" she asked, taking a sip of her apple juice.

I shook my head. "Nah, I didn't drink much last night. Just a beer or two. I wasn't really feeling it." I had thought that going out and getting drunk would have taken my mind off of Zoe and the painful feeling between my ribs, but all it did was exaggerate the feeling. I had been at the party for maybe an hour, tops, before I decided to call it quits and ran into Sophia on the porch.

"Ooh, okay." She nodded, and then quickly dropped her gaze, looking mortified.

"What?" I asked, frowning. "What's wrong?"

Sophia shielded her face with her hand. "That guy over there. He lives at the house we were at last night," she said. "I kind of made out with him and it was pretty awful so I left him in his room…"

I laughed, but there was a hollow sound to it that I couldn't explain. "That guy over there?" I jerked my head towards a boy who'd just sat down a couple tables away. "He's not facing us, you can uncover."

She sighed in relief. "Thank god. I don't actually like… know him… but I don't want to risk him recognizing me and thinking it's okay to talk to me," she explained.

"Was it really that bad?" I laughed again, fuller this time.

Sophia made a face. "You have no idea. Let's just hope for his sake that he's a better kisser when he's sober. Not that I'd ever put myself through *that* again."

"Is that why you were crying?" I teased, realizing too late that we weren't quite on that level. "Shit—sorry, wow. That was rude."

Luckily, Sophia laughed. "Probably. I don't really remember. I did throw up afterwards, though."

"Poor guy."

"Poor *me*," she corrected.

I laughed. "That's what you get for kissing drunk boys at parties, Soph. Or, well, kissing boys at all. Useless creatures, all of them."

"Pretty much, yeah. Never met one really *worth* kissing. Thus far it's always seemed to be a thing I've just… suffered through." She paused, wrinkling her nose. "God, how awful does that sound?"

I shrugged. "I mean, I'm in the same boat. So I tend to stick with kissing girls." I felt another tiny knot form in my throat when I said it. It wasn't that I was ashamed or embarrassed; I'd been out practically since I could speak and my family was *obviously* supportive – in fact, my *moms* were pretty excited that one of their kids turned out to be a lesbian, too. But there was always that twinge of fear when telling new people.

I just liked to get it out of the way before I got too attached to them.

Sophia raised her eyebrows slightly, but didn't look shocked or, well, grossed out. Which was always a good sign. I liked her. I had a feeling that we could be really good friends. And not being disgusted by my sexuality was a pretty important requirement for that.

She didn't look like she really had a response to that, which I didn't blame her for, so I decided to try to change the subject. But before I could, she spoke.

"I don't care."

My brain caught up before my mouth did. "What?" I asked, even though I knew what she was talking about.

"I don't care that you're gay. Or. Whatever you are. That you kiss girls," she fumbled a little, but she was trying. "Like, not in a 'I don't care about this big part of you that you told me about' way... in a 'it doesn't matter to me' way. If that makes sense. Sorry. It doesn't not matter. I just mean... this is coming out all... weird," she laughed sheepishly.

I laughed, "Don't worry. I gotchu. Thanks." I grinned. "I just, y'know, think you and I could be pretty good friends, Soph. So I figured I'd get it out of the way..."

She nodded. "I think so, too. Between you and me, I could use more friends here," she told me. "Or different ones, anyway. The ones I've got right now are... well. We just don't have much in common is all."

"Maybe we can look for a new pack together," I suggested. I didn't know why my mouth had decided to bring up the all too real possibility of me losing my friends over Zoe, but it did. I felt a lump forming in my chest, a few ribs down from the one already there.

Sophia raised an eyebrow. "*You* don't have any friends?" I reveled a bit in the disbelief in her voice. Did she really think I was that cool? Was it that hard to imagine me without friends?

"I mean. No. I do. But me and my girl—my ex-girlfriend—we have pretty much all the same friends, and…" I shook my head. "I broke up with her a week ago. I avoided my friends because I didn't want to tell them or talk about it, and I'm sure she's seen them and told them since. And I'm not really sure how the pieces are going to fall."

Sophia looked hesitant. Again, I'd left her with a statement that was hard to have a "right" response to. "Well, if they're gonna pick sides they're idiots. What good ever came out of that?"

I shrugged. "True. But I wouldn't blame them. It'd be hard to try to work their lives around the two of us not being together. I mean, I'd like to be friends with her someday, but I doubt she would want to be friends with me. Which is fine. But I can see how it'd be hard."

She frowned. "Well, yeah, but they're your friends, too. If they care about both of you they should want to make it work without having to cut one of you out."

"I don't know." I shook my head. "I'm sure whatever ends up happening will be for the best in the long run. I'm not *too* too worried about it. It's just. Not that great to think about."

"Sorry."

"Don't be, I'm the one who brought it up," I laughed. Nothing was particularly funny, but I wanted to lighten the mood. And I thought that maybe it'd dislodge the lump in my ribcage.

"Hey, I have to get going. I've got a paper due Monday. Do you wanna get dinner tonight or something?" Sophia asked, standing suddenly. I nodded. "Okay, cool."

"Let me get your phone number," I said, handing her my phone. "Just text yourself. What was your last name again?"

"Kalvak. Why? Know too many Sophia's to keep straight?" She smiled, handing me back my phone.

I chuckled. "Nah, I just have everyone's last name in there. It looks uneven when I've only got someone's first," I explained. "Weird, I know, whatever."

"No, I do the same thing. I was honestly going to just creep on Facebook for your last name…" She smiled, looking embarrassed. Whenever she smiled her almost black brown eyes squinted so much that they almost looked closed. And she had dimples.

"Avery."

"Annabella Avery. Alright, cool, I'll see you tonight then?" she asked.

"Yep! See you later, Soph." I watched her walk away

four
sophia jane kalvak
March 16

I had assumed that the spiders would be gone
when I woke up and was sober again, but they were
still festering hours after I awoke. Even eating
breakfast with Annabella hadn't rid me of them. I
was beginning to wonder if there was something
more to them.

  Campus was still quiet when I left the dining
commons. The sun was burning off the morning
fog, fast, and I felt tiny beads of sweat start to form
on my scalp. There were a million things I
should've done, like that damn essay, but going
back to sleep in my nice, air conditioned dorm
seemed to be the best option.

  I didn't think I was still tired until my head
hit the pillow and I felt the exhaustion wash over
me in slow, steady waves. The warmth of my

comforter pressed down on me more and more with each wave, and after only a few minutes, I found myself falling asleep.

"Sophia?" The sound of my roommate's voice pulled me out of my slumber prematurely. "Is everything alright?" She sounded concerned, but I had no idea why she would be.

"What? Yeah. I'm fine. Why?" I sat up, rubbing the sleep from my eyes. It only took a couple seconds for the spiders to wake up, too. Would I ever be rid of them? It already felt like I had put up with their crawling for a dozen lifetimes. I wrapped my arms around my stomach, wishing I could squeeze tight enough to squash them.

"Well you just left the party early and without saying goodbye. I didn't know if something happened with what's-his-face or something..." she trailed off.

"Oh, no, nothing happened. I got sick and went home.

"Alone?" I could tell that she hoped that guy—Jesus, what *was* his name?—had taken me. Emma wanted me to lose my virginity almost more than I did. It was almost a personal challenge of hers to find someone worthy of hooking up with me.

"No, some girl—Annabella—she walked be back," I told her. "She was leaving, too, and didn't think I should walk back alone."

"Annabella? As in Avery? I didn't know you two were friends."

"We're not. I mean. We weren't. We kind of are now, I guess. We're getting dinner tonight by the way, if you want to come."

"I have plans with Jared. But thanks." So they were on again this week. Great. "Does her girlfriend know? Heard she's wicked jealous. And controlling. Wouldn't wanna get mixed up in that shit," she warned.

"They broke up," I said, examining my fingernails. "Maybe that's why. Maybe she got sick of her being jealous and controlling."

"Huh. Good for her. It's not a *date* is it?" Emma smirked.

"*No,*" I said, too harsh and too quick. "No. were just friends. She's worried about losing mutual friends when they find out they broke up. So we're hanging out. I don't know." I was over explaining and I knew it, but something about her teasing set off the spiders. I felt sick.

"I'm just kidding…" Emma said slowly. "No need to freak out."

I shook my head. "I'm not freaking out. I know you were kidding. You don't think she thinks it's a date, do you?" I asked, nervous. I had no reason to be and I knew it. I didn't even *care* if Annabella thought it was a date. Well. I did. But only because I didn't want to let her down—or lose this newfound friendship. It was the first time I had made a friend independent of Emma since coming to this school in the fall.

"She's a lesbian, Sophia, not an idiot." Emma snorted. "Would you have assumed it was a date if she was a straight guy?"

"No…"

"Then she probably doesn't think it is one. Jeez, you better get your shit together if you want to actually stay friends with this girl. They don't wanna date every girl they see, babe. Not that you're not a catch or anything. Haven't you had a friend who wasn't straight before…?" I could feel her judging me. Was I that wrong? I had no idea.

I bit my lip. "My mom thinks they're all going to hell. I mean, I don't think that at all. But she does. So. No, not really. There's not too many out gay people at like, church group and shit." I forced a laugh.

"Shit, I forgot you were like, insanely sheltered," Emma said.

"I wasn't *that* sheltered. I had cable." I laughed.

Emma kicked her shoes off and tucked her feet under herself. "Oh, yeah, and I'm sure you had about eight thousand parental blocks, right? So you and your little prayer circle could only watch like, Full House and Fox News."

"*Hey*, we were allowed to watch Zoboomafo, too," I joked.

She laughed. "Wow, okay, I stand corrected. Clearly you were raised to be even worldlier than I was."

We lapsed into a comfortable silence then. Emma was playing some game on her phone while I laid back down and tried to cut off a headache I felt growing behind my eyes. I always seemed to get headaches when awoken by something that wasn't my body's natural alarm clock. As if my brain was angry at me or the world or whatever external force I allowed myself to come in contact with for robbing it of its sleep. I hoped that if I could fall back asleep before it got too bad, the headache wouldn't follow me for the rest of the day.

Just as I was about to fall back asleep, Emma spoke. "You don't mind if Jared hangs out here tonight, do you? I don't think he's going to spend the night or anything. But his roommate's girlfriend is in town 'til tomorrow and they asked for some privacy."

I rolled over to face the wall, suppressing a groan. "I mean… I'm not thrilled about it, but fine." I didn't want to be that bitchy roommate who said she couldn't have her boyfriend over, but *god* I hated Jared. He treated her like shit. But at least if they hung out here, I would be able to defend her if he did something shitty.

"I wish you would just give him a chance."

"I did. And he turned out to be garbage. But this is your room too, so I'm not gonna tell you no. Do you want me gone so you guys can have some privacy, too?" I asked, squeezing my eyes shut. I hoped she said no. Mostly because I wanted to hold Jared accountable, but also because I had nowhere else to really *go*.

I could hear her tapping on the touch screen of her phone. "What? No. You can stay. We're just gonna watch a movie or something, probably," she said. "Are you sure it's okay? I don't want you to feel awkward. Maybe Annabella could come hang out, too. Or I could have Jared text that guy from last night—he seemed really into you, Sophia."

This time, I couldn't hold in my groan. "I don't think so. He's not my type. Plus I kind of ditched him... I told him I was going to get a beer and then never came back. Left him upstairs in his bedroom."

"*Sophia*!" Emma laughed, but I could hear her slapping her hand to her forehead. "Not your type? Really? He's wicked hot. Why did you leave?" She sounded genuinely confused. "I thought your goal for the semester or whatever was to get laid. Change your mind?"

I didn't want to have this conversation. "He was an awful kisser."

"He was drunk, honey."

"Well, still."

"Alright then..." I could practically hear her eyebrow raising in that judgmental way of hers.

It was quiet for a minute. "I didn't change my mind. I just don't want him," I said finally.

"The semester is practically over. I don't see why you feel the need to rush this like, at all, but you're almost at your deadline." Emma had never understood, of course. She'd chocked my goal up to external pressure when, really, there was none. There were no people around me pressuring me to have sex. Really, most were doing the opposite. My mom. My grandmother. Emma, when it came down to it.

It wasn't even that I was overwhelmingly sexually frustrated, either. There was just this ever-growing ping of worry that maybe there was a reason no one ever wanted to date me or have sex with me. Maybe it wasn't because I was always more interested in something else to form any kind of romantic or sexual relationship. Maybe I was just sexually repugnant.

And the more time you have to think about that kind of stuff, the more real it is. And the more daunting actually *having sex* feels.

I just wanted to get it out of the way, truth be told. But Emma, who had lost her virginity to Jared about three and a half years ago, never got that.

"I'm not rushing anything. It's not a deadline. It's a goal. Something to aim for. Not an end all be all."

"If you say so…"

I squeezed my eyes shut tighter. "I'll see if Annabella wants to hang out maybe. After eating two meals with me in one day she might get sick of me, don't you think?"

"Probably. Heaven knows I do."

"I love you too, asshole."

"Oh shush, you know I love you, baby. I'm just kidding. I could never get sick of you." Her phone buzzed. "I'll catch you later though, I have to go meet this girl at the library to review her midterm essay." Her bed creaked as she stood up. "There's migraine medicine in my top desk drawer, by the way. Feel better. Get some sleep or something." I waited until I heard the heavy door slam shut before I rolled over onto my back.

She always seemed to know when something was off with me. And she almost always knew how to fix it.

I wondered what she'd recommend for the spiders.

By the time four o'clock rolled around, I was considering cancelling with Annabella. My headache was still pounding in my temples and behind my eyes. I didn't manage to get any sleep at all and Emma's medicine barely took the edge off. And even though I was awake all day, I accomplished almost nothing with my essay. I still had six pages to go.

Just as I was about to take my phone out and text her, it chimed.

Annabella: are we still on for dinner? how does 5 sound? ☺

My fingers hovered above the screen, torn between my headache and my desire to go. *It's not like sitting around did anything to get rid of it in the first place...*

Sophia: five sounds great, see you then!

I hit send, swallowing down a lump in my throat. I tossed my phone to the other end of my bed, not wanting to look at it anymore. Was the exclamation mark too enthusiastic? Five *sounds great*? Did I reply too quickly?

I'd never sounded so stupid over text, I was sure of it. I felt a pit open up in my stomach, empty and gaping and void of spiders or eyelashes. What if she thought I was overeager or stupid or, or, or?

There was no reason for me to be so anxious, but I was. I wanted Annabella to think I was cool. Which I wasn't. Which I never had been or would be. But I wanted her to believe it. I wanted her to be my friend. I wanted her to like me. Because *I* thought *she* was cool.

God, was it lame of me to think she was cool? Even the word "cool" sounded desperate and uncool.

I laid back down, shoving my face into the pillow. Maybe it'd be better if I just asphyxiated myself. I was an idiot. Who over the age of fifteen was still worried about being perceived as "cool"? A loud groan escaped my lips, but it was mostly absorbed by the pillow's stuffing.

My phone chimed. I pretended I didn't hear it. The hollow feeling in my stomach migrated upwards into my chest, nestling itself somewhere between my heart and my sternum. I kicked my phone off the bed, and then immediately regretted it.

It probably wasn't Annabella, but then what if it was? I didn't want to answer right away and seem too eager to be her friend. But what if it was important? What if she didn't want to meet at five anymore? What if she wanted to meet at six or seven or not at all?

Someone needed to hit me. I was spiraling. It was ridiculous and embarrassing, even though no one was there to see it but me. I tried to pretend I didn't think any of those thoughts. Tried lying to myself. Tried pretending I didn't care. And then, slowly, I got up and got my phone.

Mom: spring break starts the 22nd right? I will pick you up at noon, be ready. did you get your grandmother a birthday present yet? it is the 24th remember?

I wanted to throw my phone back on the floor. I was being such an idiot. What was I even freaking out about? I tapped out a quick reply to my mom, then went back and read Annabella's text again.

Sophia: okay. and no I didn't get her anything, I was going to take her to dinner at that restaurant down the street that she likes.

Mom replied almost instantly. I flipped back to our text, painfully aware of the minutes I still had remaining before I could go to dinner. It was sitting around doing nothing that made me anxious.

Mom: good idea! she will love that. the two of you never spend any time one-on-one.

I flipped the phone over, screen down. It was almost quarter past four. Almost. I still had a good half hour before it was a reasonable time to leave. And it would only take me five, *maybe* ten minutes to get dressed and ready, considering all I really had to do was swap my pajama pants for the jeans I'd had on earlier. Would it be weird to show up in a completely different outfit than what I wore to breakfast? Would she even notice? Why did I care?

I was early, she was late. I sat at the same table we'd eaten breakfast at and texted her to let her know where to find me. I figured it was easier than sitting somewhere else and making her look for me.

I ate slowly while I was waiting for her, mostly just pushing my food around on the pale blue plate. The food at school was normally decent, but today it tasted like sand in my mouth. I wasn't feeling it.

Annabella showed up about fifteen minutes late, plate of food in hand. *Maybe she got stuck in the line. They were pretty long.* Why was I justifying it? Fifteen minutes wasn't a big deal. It was dinner at the dining commons for god's sake. I was being ridiculous and I knew it—but what else was new?

"Hey, Soph!" She smiled cheerfully as she sat down. I smiled back. "Long time no see. How was the rest of your day?"

"Uneventful. I hung out with my roommate for a little but mostly I just sat around. I got some of my essay done but not much." God, I was so boring. "What about you?"

Annabella took a sip of her water. "I didn't really do anything, either. Studied a little. Hung out with my sister for a little. Watched some Friends reruns." From what she described, her day was about as interesting as mine, but it didn't seem so pathetic when she said it. I kicked myself mentally—and then kicked every one of my ancestors—for being born so boring and plain.

"Oh nice. I love Friends." *I love Friends. Jesus, Sophia, who doesn't?*

Annabella nodded. "Yeah me too. Oh, and I read this book about Incan mythology that my moms sent me."

"Incan mythology?"

"Yeah. One of my moms is super into like… indigenous mythological stuff. Nothing Greco-Roman, but literally everything else." She laughed. "And the other is obsessed with making sure my sisters don't 'forget our heritage' or something like that. We're all adopted from Argentina, and I'm pretty sure they've given us every book on straight up Argentinian mythology. So apparently she's moved onto the Incas." She shrugged. "I mean, I'm not all that into it, but it makes them happy. And it's kind of interesting."

"That's really cool. My dad used to talk about Inuit mythology and stuff all the time when I was younger. My mom *hated* it," I told her. "My dad's myths and legends are the only things I really remember about him, to be honest. He died when I was eight. So that's where my connection to his culture ended, really. You're lucky your moms want you to be connected to yours."

Annabella made that face everyone did when they found out my dad was dead. Lips pursed together, slight frown, wide eyes. "I'm sorry, Soph."

"It was eleven years ago. It's okay." I shrugged.

She cleared her throat. "Why did your mom hate it so much?" she asked.

"Oh, I don't know. She's really Catholic, so she considered it all blasphemy pretty much. And my dad's favorite myth was about Sedna and Qailertetang. Who, depending on who you ask, were lesbians." I shrugged. "In my dad's version she was the daughter of Anguta, the creator god, and she refused to marry any of the suitors he presented her with. She said she'd rather marry a dog than a man. So her dad got pissed and tried to drown her, only she clung to the boat. So he cut off her fingers and they fell into the ocean and became like, seals and whales and otters and stuff.

She sank to the bottom of the ocean but she didn't die, instead she became the goddess of the three Inuit underworlds. Qailertetang was a goddess who could control the weather and cares for the sea-mammals. I don't really remember much else of the story, but they fell in love somehow."

I did remember the rest, of course, but all the sudden I became too-aware of my voice and how much I was talking. "Sorry," I said meekly. "Kinda went off on a tangent there."

"No, it's fine, that's really interesting actually," Annabella assured me. "What do you believe?"

"Me? I don't know. Nothing really. They're nice stories, I guess…" I shrugged. "I was brought up Catholic but I never really bought it. My mom thinks I go to church still, though." I laughed a little. "Why, what do you believe?" This seemed like such a weird conversation to be having so early on in our friendship. But then again, up until recently it was never a conversation I had the opportunity to *have*. Everyone I knew back home was Catholic or pretending to be. Maybe people normally discussed stuff like this. Maybe I was the weird one. Although, I had been living with Emma since August and we'd been talking since last January and it'd never come up with us.

"A little bit of everything, I guess. I've been to six kinds of churches, two synagogues, and a mosque between my freshman and senior year. My moms were on this religious kick where they wanted to 'find themselves' or something. Nothing fully stuck but everything left a couple pieces behind." She put her fork down, having finished eating, and I realized that I hadn't even taken a bite since she'd arrived.

"Oh, wow, did anything stick with them?" I wondered what it was like, being exposed to so many faiths. My mom was quick enough to dismiss other branches of Christianity, let alone Islam or Judaism or, god forbid, anything else. And I'd never even given it a second thought, really. Maybe I'd find something there that I never found in Catholicism. Maybe my mom was afraid of that. Maybe that's why she never let me even learn about anything different. What other reason could she have?

Annabella shook her head. "Nah, I don't think so. Ma is more into religion as stories than truths. And Mom only really did it because Ma wanted to. She was never that interested, really," she explained. "It was a good experience, though, I guess. Can't know what you believe until you know what you don't." She shrugged. "Anyway, I don't think any one religion knows it all. Or has everything—or even close to—right. I don't believe anyone is more right or wrong than the next person when it comes to faith. The way I see it, if it makes you happy, doesn't hurt anyone, and helps you sleep better at night—how can it be wrong?" She sounded convinced, but something like fear or worry flashed across her face. It widened her eyes and hardened her brow.

I nodded slowly. I wanted to reply, to keep the conversation going, but I was at a loss. She made me feel kind of dumb, but in the best way. The kind of dumb that's desperate to know more I wanted to know enough about life, about everything, to keep up with her. To keep her talking forever. She was so interesting. I didn't understand it. But I knew I would never get tired of hearing what she thought and what she had to say.

"So, anyway," Annabella said after a few moments, mistaking my silence for disinterest. "Any big plans for tonight? I'm not keeping you, am I?"

"No, not really," I said, too quickly. "My roommate is having her boyfriend over to watch a movie and invited me, but I'm not too eager to deal with him." My stomach fluttered. "What about you?"

"Absolutely nothing. Unless you wanna do something?" she asked. "It's okay if you're sick of me or something. We've seen a lot of each other today—I won't be offended."

I bit back my desire to tell her I could never be sick of her. "You mean you're not sick of *me* yet?"

"Nah, I could probably tolerate you for another couple hours." She winked. "So is that a yes?"

"Anything to keep me from Jared," I said. "So what did you have in mind?"

"I hadn't thought that far ahead." Annabella shrugged. "I just knew I wanted to spend more time with you…" She stopped, looking uncertain. "I mean, like… oh, whatever. We have good conversations. I like being around you—even when you're too drunk to walk home. I told you before—I think we could be good friends is all."

"No, it's okay, I know what you mean. I feel the same. You just *know* with some people, y'know?" I was relieved to hear that it wasn't just me. That she wanted me around as much as I wanted her around. Maybe it was weird but I just knew somehow that our friendship had potential. I was never more certain of anything. I was never more drawn to someone. And even if I was wrong, she fascinated me.

Maybe it was weird, but if we both felt the same way, what did it matter?

"So, any ideas?"

"Well. We could watch a movie. Or hang at the student center. Or sit on the quad… it's still pretty warm, I think." I shrugged. "I don't know. I'm down for pretty much anything. So I guess it's up to you."

Annabella hesitated, looking thoughtful. "We could get a blanket and go sit on the quad for a while. While it's still nice. I think my roommate has people over tonight to study."

"Sure, that sounds good," I said, careful to not sound overeager. "Let's do that." I stood, picking up my practically untouched plate of food. Annabella glanced at it before she stood, too. "Wasn't hungry." I shrugged again.

She shrugged, too, then headed for the dish drop. After watching her for a moment, I followed close behind.

five

annabella morgan avery
March 16

It was colder outside than we had expected it to
be. It wasn't unbearable, but it was chilly. I asked
Sophia if she still wanted to lay on the quad,
though, and she did. So when we stopped at my
dorm for a blanket, I grabbed two sweatshirts just in
case. When I came back outside, I offered one to
her, and she put it on almost instantly.

We didn't talk as we crossed campus from
my building to the quad. We were walking so close
together that our arms were practically touching.
And with me a step or two ahead of her, it looked
like our elongated shadows were holding hands. I
watched them shrink and grow with each lamppost
we walked by.

The grass on the quad was slightly damp,
but not uncomfortably so. Once we spread the

blanket, we could hardly feel it. We laid side by side on our stomachs; me, propped up on my elbows, her, resting her head on her arm. She closed her eyes. For a minute, I thought she was falling asleep, but then she spoke.

"Do you believe in aliens?"

"What? I guess so. Do you?"

She nodded, eyes still shut. "Not like, little green men with big black eyes but. There's gotta be something else out there right?" she asked. "What about ghosts?"

"Definitely. You?"

"No. Afterlife?"

"Heaven yes, Hell no."

"God?"

"Maybe."

"Maybe is a good answer." Sophia rolled over onto her back. "Why Heaven and not Hell?" she asked. She raised her arms up, a cross between stretching and just reaching, before crossing them over her eyes.

I frowned. I'd never really considered it. "Well I don't want to believe in a God that would punish someone for all eternity," I said.

"Some people deserve it. And you said you maybe believe in God."

"I'd like to think that those people just cease to exist. Just the really bad ones. The murderers and the rapists and the pedophiles. I maybe believe in a God who lets like, tax evaders and petty thieves and people who don't use their turn signal into Heaven." Sophia laughed. "It's more of a hope than a belief," I admitted. "I can't imagine what dying is like if there's nothing. And I don't like the idea of something I can't imagine."

"I think it's probably just like sleeping."

"Without dreaming?"

"Maybe."

"And you just never wake up?"

Sophia hesitated. "Well, presumably. But maybe you do. Maybe you sleep for a while and rest and then… y'know, whatever. You come back as a bear or a fruit fly or a ghost or you go to Heaven or wherever." She sounded thoughtful. "I don't know, I've never died."

I laughed. "Fair enough." A gust of wind swept the quad, making the hairs on my arms stand up even under my sweatshirt. I took the corner of the blanket and rolled with it, cocooning myself in it.

"Cold?" Sophia asked, looking over at me. "We can go inside if you want. If your roommate still has people over, you're welcome to my room," she offered.

"Nah, I'm okay. Unless you want to?" part of me did want to go inside, but I didn't want to make Sophia if she didn't want to. I wasn't that concerned with it.

"It is getting a little chilly," she said. "Probably not the best idea to lay outside at night in March." She laughed a little, the sound getting lost somewhere in the sleeve of my sweatshirt. I caught myself hoping it would stay there, lodged in the fabric. "Jared is probably still going to be there, but we can go back to my room." She rolled onto her stomach, propping herself up on her elbows.

"That sounds good. Hang on, you've got something in your hair," I told her, reaching over and gently pulling the long strands of dried grass from her black hair. "I think I got them all. Turn?" She did. I pulled another piece out. "Okay, now I think I got them all. The bigger ones anyway." I unwrapped myself, sitting up.

Sophia ran her fingers through her hair, untangling it and dislodging the smaller pieces of grass that I had missed. I did the same with my own hair, but my fingers just got caught in the curls near the end. It wasn't worth trying to rip through.

I looked back over at Sophia, who was standing now. The lights on the outside of academic building behind her where shining on her back, giving her an almost angelic glow. A hazy gray feeling began to fester in my stomach, and I looked away. She was beautiful. But she was straight. And I had literally broken up with Zoe a week ago. What was wrong with me?

I was just sad and confused and alone.

I made the conscious choice to stop. I didn't want to think of Sophia as anything but a friend. And so I didn't. Because that was what I needed and wanted; a friend.

Her roommate's boyfriend was still there. It was about eight o'clock when we walked in, and the two of them were snuggled up together on her bed. Sophia murmured a quiet 'hello' to Emma. When she looked at me, all I had to offer was a tight lipped smile. I wasn't usually uncomfortable with new people but, for whatever reason, I was then.

There was some sort of tension in the room that felt familiar but unnamable.

They were watching some movie I didn't recognize. A straight, white couple was kissing onscreen, which gave absolutely nothing about the movie away. Emma's boyfriend—Jared?—looked engrossed in it, but she looked distracted.

Sophia sat down on her bed and pulled the blanket over her crossed legs. "Sit down, make yourself at home," she told me. I kicked off my shoes and sat down next to her, knees almost touching. She offered me some of the blanket, which I gratefully accepted, and turned to watch the movie.

But I couldn't focus.

Zoe and I had a film studies class together on Tuesday afternoon. She had skipped it last week, but I didn't expect to be that lucky this time around. She would be there. She wouldn't skip twice in a row.

I walked into class with knives in my throat and chest. It felt strange walking into class early and alone. Zoe and I always used to get lunch before it, which usually ended in us being a couple minutes late. The room was pretty much empty, save for a boy and a girl sitting on the other side of the room. I considered sitting in my usual seat, but I didn't want a turf war.

She could sit in the back, left corner like we usually did. And I would sit in the front right corner. As far away as possible. I didn't want any confrontation with her whatsoever. Especially not when I still felt so guilty about it all.

I wasn't wrong. But I felt it.

People filtered in slowly over the next twenty minutes, quietly filling the movie theatre style seats. Zoe was the very last person to walk in. I didn't look at her, but I felt her stare. It sent shivers up and down my spine.

The professor arrived fifteen minutes late, as usual, and started praising the class on how well we did on our last unit exam. After a couple minutes of that, he lowered the projection screen and started today's movie.

I watched it, I really did, but I couldn't hold the information in my head. Who was that girl? What was his name? How did they know each other? Why were they in that room? Why did she just shoot him? I couldn't focus. The film was going straight through me, I couldn't process it. All I could think about was Zoe, sitting quietly in the back of the room. I swore I could still feel her eyes on the back of my head.

God, I didn't want her to talk to me. But I did. I missed her. I wanted to talk to her. But at the same time, I couldn't stand the thought of it. I knew it was a terrible idea to talk to her. But I knew it was something I needed to do eventually.

I was tearing myself apart over something I knew was going to happen. I knew Zoe. She was going to talk to me unless I managed to apparate out of the room. Given my lack of a Hogwarts letter, that didn't seem too likely.

My stomach hurt.

I briefly considered leaving early, but what would avoiding her accomplish? It was going to happen. It had to. I had to. I had to. I had to.

Maybe if I thought it enough times, I'd be more okay with it. It wasn't likely. I was never good with confrontation when it came to girlfriends. Anyone else? Sure. Bring it on. I knew how to stand up for myself. I was calm and collected. But with girls I liked or, in Zoe's case, loved? Forget it.

I was already starting to shake.

Class ended and I didn't move.
Students left the room and I didn't move.
Zoe stood in front of me and I didn't move.

I didn't even look at her. The knives were sticking into my chest and my throat and my eyes and I wanted to look at her, to acknowledge her, but I couldn't do it.

I stared down at her knees. I couldn't bring myself to look at any other part of her. She was just standing there. Staring at me. Waiting for me to speak. So I stared at her knees, which seemed like the least hostile part of her at first.

She was wearing shorts and her legs were so paper white and I knew that in any other situation she would be embarrassed that I was looking at them because she hated people seeing her pale, pale legs no matter how much I told her that they were beautiful and soft and strong and I was spiraling away from the situation at light speed and soon I would be galaxies away from her and this building and this school and this state and this planet.

"Annabella." A knife in my throat slid in deeper. She never called me by my full name. I was always Anna to her. The way she said it made me feel like a stranger. I wanted to throw up. "We need to talk." We needed so many things but I couldn't help but think that talking wasn't one of them. We could talk forever and it wouldn't undo what I did, what I wanted, what I felt. It wouldn't even *explain* any of it.

I could hear the distinct sound of my heart breaking all over again. I knew it was mine this time, because she seemed so steady and so strong. I was melting into the chair. "What do we need to talk about, Zoe?" My mouth was a desert, I couldn't believe the words managed to crawl out.

"Us," she said matter-of-factly. "I don't want us to be over. We're not over." Her voice was stern, level. She wasn't asking. She was telling. She wasn't emotional. She was certain. This was right. She was right. We weren't over.

I swallowed the sand in my mouth. "We're over, Zoe. We are. Really. There is no more us. I'm sorry."

"No."

"What do you mean *no*? This isn't a two person decision. You can't debate your way into a relationship." The knives fell out of my throat and chest, but a new one was lodged in my head. I felt the pain bloom outwards, flowing from the center to all regions of my brain.

"Don't I get a say?" She almost sounded hurt, but not in any real way. She sounded hurt like she did when she was teasing me. When she wanted me to tell her I loved her after an argument. When she lost a game. When it was my turn to decide where we went on a date, but she wanted to do something else. When she wanted something I didn't want to give her.

She wasn't hurt, she was upset that she wasn't getting her way.

The ache in my ribs returned. "No, Zoe, you don't get a say. You really don't. I broke up with you. I was the only one who got a say. If you broke up with me, then you'd get the say. See how that works?" I blinked the daggers out of my eyes and looked up at her. For the first time since I met her, her beauty didn't faze me. I barely even recognized her.

"It's not *fair*." I half expected her to stomp her foot. Had she always been so childish?

I stared at her until she looked away. "Fair? Jesus, Zoe, nothing's fair. Life isn't fair and it never has been. But we're over. You're going to have to accept that."

"But I love you."

I stood up, forcing her to take a couple steps back. "And I'm sorry about that, Zoe. I really am. But that doesn't change anything. I can't be with you anymore."

"You still haven't even told me *why*. You said you still loved me. If you love me, why can't you be with me? Why can't we work this out? I want to work it out, Anna. And if you don't tell me where we went wrong, I can't fix it." She was staring at the floor now, her blue eyes unreadable. I couldn't help but wonder if she was playing me again. If she was just trying to get her way again.

"We stopped working. It didn't feel right anymore. I don't want to be with you anymore. God, Zoe, I told you I don't know what it is. I just know that we shouldn't be together. I can't do it anymore and I won't. It doesn't matter why I broke up with you because I did and it's over and I don't *want* you to fix it, can't you understand that?" I wanted to tear my hair out at the roots. "I don't want you Zoe. I don't. You need to understand that." I hated myself so much, but it needed to be said. She wouldn't listen otherwise. She wouldn't get it otherwise. I could feel the tears spring up in my eyes, and then sliding hot and sticky down my cheeks, but I couldn't and wouldn't take it back. "I don't want you anymore, Zoe."

She turned away from me. I didn't know if she was crying or not, but some sick part of me hoped that she was. I tried to tell myself that I wanted that because then I'd know she knew it was done, but I didn't believe it. A broken, angry part of me that I couldn't identify or explain just wanted her to hurt, too.

"Okay. Fine. Fuck you, Annabella. Fuck you." She looked back at me and her eyes were dry. "You want to be over? Fine. We're fucking over. Are you fucking happy now?" She stormed out of the room, leaving a trail of pure animosity in the air behind her.

"No," I said, but she was already gone.

six
sophia jane kalvak
March 19

Emma and I spent an unexpected snow day in
our room, in her bed, watching a movie. The wind
was absolutely howling outside. Thick flurries of
white were quickly burying the still sleeping college
town. Around five in the morning, we were awoken
by automated texts from the school and we hadn't
managed to fall back asleep since.

　　She had picked out the movie. It was some
children's cartoon about a Russian girl that I was
supposed to be familiar with but wasn't. I tried
explaining to her that my mother wasn't big on
anything that wasn't overtly Christian—and there
were necromancers and spells and ghosts in this
movie. Plus, from the looks of it, it would've scared
the living hell out of me when I was younger.

But it was Emma's favorite and she insisted that no snow day was complete without kid's movies.

About halfway through the movie, my stomach started growling. "Em, do you want breakfast?" Her eyes were locked on the screen. A man was morphing into a bat onscreen and I found myself unable to believe that this was an actual children's movie. How did they not have nightmares every night?

"Huh? I'm not going outside if that's what you're asking."

"No, I have like, hot chocolate and oatmeal and stuff. Do you want some?" I offered. "I'll go make it." It was barely seven am but I was already stir crazy. I needed to leave the room more than anything.

She shrugged. "If you're gonna make some for you, I'll have some. Thanks." She smiled at me, but she was still watching the movie. I slid off the bed, putting on a pair of beat up black flip flops that were mainly used in the showers, and grabbed the food out of my closet.

"I'll be right back."

The kitchen was essentially just a closet with a microwave and a sink, but it was enough. I filled the little oatmeal cups up with water to the pre-drawn line and put them in the microwave. While they spun around under the light bulb, absorbing all the heat and radiation, I counted the bricks in the wall. When there was one minute left, I counted how many times I breathed. That was easier said than done, seeing as I always switched to manual breathing when I even so much as *thought* about the fact that I was breathing.

When the oatmeal was done, I took a cup and filled it up with water. Emma had a Keurig in our room, but I didn't want to go back just yet. I put the cup of water in the microwave and turned back around.

I found myself wondering what Annabella was up to. If she and her roommate were having a movie day, too. If she even liked her roommate. Or the snow. I wondered if she had talked to her ex-girlfriend at all, but immediately stopped that thought in its tracks. Something about it made the spiders in my stomach act up again, just when I thought I'd finally escaped them.

The microwave beeped loudly, slicing into my daze, and I grabbed everything and made my way back to my room. It was a pain in the ass to try to put my code in with my hands full, but I managed, and quickly put everything down on my dresser.

Emma was still engrossed in her movie, barely even glancing at me as I handed her the oatmeal. If it was anyone else, I'd be annoyed. But movies were her favorite thing in the world. Especially animated movies. Which made it more endearing than annoying. I was honored to be acknowledged at all, honestly.

I ate my oatmeal while I mixed our hot chocolate. I felt very separate from my body in a way I couldn't really explain. Almost like I was standing behind myself, watching my every move through a thin curtain. I chalked it up to tiredness, even though I never felt more fully awake.

When the powder was sufficiently dissolved, I handed Emma a mug and sat back down beside her, pulling the blankets over me. I was completely lost with the movie now, and I didn't particularly care to find my way again.

I took a quick sip of hot chocolate, giving myself third degree burns on my tongue and mouth. As I set the cup down on the dresser next to Emma's bed, her phone buzzed.

"Can you hand me that?"

"Yeah, sure," I said, handing her the phone.

She tapped away on the screen for a second. "It's Jared. He wants to hang out." Emma handed me her oatmeal and stood up. "I'll see you later, okay?"

"Yeah, sure, later," I said, trying not to sound too disappointed. I *almost* felt bad for how much I wished they would just break up (for the eighteen hundredth time). Emma and I never had any good, quality time together when they were on. She was always texting him or calling him or upset about him or leaving me to go be with him. I was jealous and it was petty, but to be fair, he was an awful person.

"Love you." She kissed my forehead as she buttoned her jeans.

"Love you, too. Bye." Emma put on her boots and left. The door closed loudly behind her, sucking all the sound out of the room. It felt quiet enough to hear my own blood flowing, even though

I knew it wasn't *really*. There was just too much empty space to fill.

The movie was pretty much over, but I didn't know what happened during any of it. I changed it to cable and put on some random cartoon I'd never seen but apparently was very popular.

I didn't pay any attention, though. I couldn't. I kept catching myself compulsively checking my phone for texts. I didn't know what I was waiting for or who I expected to text me, but every couple minutes or so I'd find myself unlocking my phone again only to turn the screen back off and put it down.

It wasn't like there was anyone even *to* text me, either. Emma was with Jared. My 'friends' were more hers, and I never really talked to them. Annabella and I texted on and off on Monday, but she hadn't answered the two texts I sent her yesterday. I tried to tell myself that I hadn't done anything wrong—what *could* I have done?—but there was still a nagging feeling. Maybe that was why I couldn't put my phone down. I wanted that validation. That 'we're okay' kind of affirmation.

It didn't matter. We barely knew each other. But at the same time, it did matter. I did care. I wanted to be her friend so, so badly. I wanted *a* friend so, so badly.

My phone buzzed and my heart almost stopped. I tried to laugh it off, embarrassed even though I was alone. I unlocked my phone.

Just an email. Spam, no less.

I put the phone down on my dresser and crawled underneath my blankets. The TV faded into background noise until I no longer understood what the characters onscreen were saying. I squeezed my eyes shut and made a conscious decision to go to sleep and not look at my phone unless it actually went off. And even then, I decided, I would wait so my response didn't seem overeager.

Overthinking everything. Drowning in it.

I pressed my face harder into the pillow.

It was still snowing when I woke up, but the piles on the ground didn't look any higher. I thought for a second that I hadn't actually fallen asleep at all, but a quick look at Emma's clock told me that it was almost noon. The sunlight streaming through the window felt too hot for a snowy day like this. I threw the blankets off of myself and rolled onto my back, staring up at the ceiling.

My phone was still sitting on the dresser, silent.

I should check it, I've been asleep. Emma might have texted me.

I said I wouldn't look unless I heard it.

But I was asleep. It could've gone off. I wouldn't have heard.

I mean it probably didn't but what if—

My phone buzzed, interrupting my internal debate. I hadn't gotten any texts while I was asleep, but Emma had just sent one.

```
Emma: hey, there's a big snowball
fight going on on the quad. you
should come! and after we're going
```

to the dining commons- they have
baked mac tonight ☺

    I wasn't really one for snowball fights, or
snow in general, but I needed to get out of my own
head. I texted Emma back a quick "okay, I'll see
you in a bit" and dragged myself out of bed.

    I got dressed slowly, replacing each article
of clothing as I took it off. I was plagued by a cross
between not wanting to see myself naked and being
too cold to stand the few minutes that any part of
me was uncovered. The double whammy of
discomfort was almost enough for me to want to
text Emma back and tell her never mind, but I
managed.

    I felt formless in an oversized sweatshirt and
sweatpants, but I wasn't going to wear jeans in the
snow. I pulled on a thick pair of blue knee-high
socks and shoved my feet in my boots.

    Examining myself in the mirror didn't make
me feel any better. I looked large and lumpy in the
baggy clothes. My skin looked washed out under
the fluorescent lighting, like someone had coated it
in a soft layer of chalk dust. My long, black hair
looked too shiny. My dark eyes looked too narrow.
I wished for the thousandth time that I looked more
like my mom and less like my dad.

    My mother was a white redhead with the
greenest eyes I'd ever seen. She was short and
petite. I was tall and thick and brown and looked so
different from her that when I was younger I was
convinced that she wasn't my real mom. My dad
told me I was beautiful, the spitting image of my

late grandmother. When he was alive, I could at least see myself in him. We looked related when we went out in public. And then he died and it was just me and mom, and we never really looked like a family again.

She told me it was good that I looked like him, because it was all she had left of him. I thought that was selfish.

I closed my eyes and turned away from the mirror, pushing back all the negative thoughts. For the most part, I had managed to move past them over the years. On some days, I even liked the way I looked. But everyone had their bad days, I supposed.

It wasn't as cold out as the snow had led me to believe, but it was still too cold for me. There was easily forty people on the quad, throwing snowballs, and I couldn't find Emma or any of her friends in the fray. I circled the quad once, searching for a familiar face, and then resigned myself to sitting on the stairs to the res hall next to it.

I watched the snowball fight for I don't know how long. I tried to pay attention and try to see if I could spot Emma, but my mind kept drifting elsewhere. I felt detached and tired in a way I couldn't really explain; I couldn't really focus enough to be tired, but only because my brain was so exhausted. I felt the now-familiar crawling sensation in my abdomen, but I was distanced from it. It was happening to someone else and they were vividly describing it to me. I didn't have a stomach to fill with spiders.

I knew that I should have been worried that I was dissociating so much lately, but I couldn't grab on to the feeling. It would pass, I was sure.

It took some effort, but I managed to push through the fog enough to focus on the buzzing bodies on the quad again. In fact, I did so just in time to see Emma emerge from the masses and head towards me.

"Sophia! Don't you want to join in?" She asked. Her cheeks were red and shiny and her hazel eyes looked bright. It had been a while since I'd seen her look this genuinely happy. Jared always seemed to take that out of her.

"Nah, I'd rather watch. You go have fun though, Emma." I told her with a plastic-feeling smile. I was surprised that she hadn't noticed how... off I'd been. Knowing her though, she had noticed, and she was just waiting for the right time to force it all out of me. The thought almost made me laugh. What was there to force out?

She looked skeptical. "Well, I'm not gonna force you. But don't feel like you have to just sit here and watch. If you wanna leave that's okay," she assured me. "Oh—before I forget. Elise and Allison are throwing Friday, you down?"

I nodded. "Yeah, sure, why not." A better question would be 'why.' After my miserable experience at the last party, I wasn't too keen on going to another. But I liked Allison, at least (Elise was another story), and I didn't have to drink as much as I did last time. Emma was right—the semester was almost over and I was no closer to getting laid now than I was my freshman year of high school. Time to revise the plan.

I stifled a laugh.

"Alright cool! I'll let them know you're coming. It should be fun. Nothing too big, don't worry. Their place isn't as big as the guys' house." Emma reassured me. "Seriously though—you don't have to stay out here if you don't want to join. I thought you'd want to, that's why I invited you. Don't freeze your ass off for no reason." She touched my arm. "Okay?"

"Yeah, okay, mom." I rolled my eyes.

Emma laughed, then turned and jogged back into the mess of people. It didn't take long for me to lose sight of her again.

I took my phone out of my sweatshirt pocket and opened my text to Annabella. She hadn't answered me back since Monday, and I was trying not to let it bother me. I was anxious about texting her again when she still hadn't responded, but what was the worst that could happen?

Sophia: hey, Emma's friends are throwing on Friday night if you're interested

I hit send and held my breath, staring at the screen. I didn't even know if Annabella *liked* parties. Sure she went last week but she left early. And what if she *was* ignoring me on purpose? I didn't want to look pathetic. I didn't want to look stupid. But I felt it. I was such an—

My phone went off.

Annabella: sounds good! sorry I
haven't texted you back. I'm super
busy. wanna get dinner tomorrow
night around 5?

I inhaled deeply, letting the relief fill my
lungs, and texted her back a quick "see you then!"
before shoving my phone back in my pocket. As if
not looking at it could keep me from my ceaseless
overthinking.

seven

annabella morgan avery
March 20

It had been ten days since I had broken up with Zoe. And, subsequently, ten days since I had seen any of my friends. I woke up that morning with the knowledge that I had to talk to them that day. Just texting them out of the blue felt cheap, though. And I didn't want to chance running into Zoe by seeking them out in their usual places.

So I did the cheap thing and texted one of them. Aliyah. Who, out of the group, I was closest with. That wasn't really saying much—as they were Zoe's friends first and foremost—but Aliyah and I had hung out on our own a couple times. I considered us friends outside of Zoe. It was time to see if she thought the same.

I was surprised at how quickly Aliyah responded back. And even more surprised that she agreed to meet me in the student center in half an hour.

I dropped my phone on my chest and covered my face with my hands. I could've left right then, but I always felt awkward when I was alone in the student center. Being alone didn't bother me often, but something about being the only person alone in a sea of people coming and going with their friends made me feel self-conscious.

My eyelids felt heavy and weak. I had only just woken up, but they were already ready to close again. I rubbed the heels of my hands into them, hard, and tried to squash the sleep out of them. Of course, it didn't do any good.

I sat up, legs crossed underneath me, and twisted my spine to crack it. I felt stiff after a too-long night of sleep. While that loosened me up a bit, I still felt knotted up both physically and emotionally. What if Aliyah didn't want my apology? What if I was too late? What if they'd all made up their minds?

They were Zoe's friends first. I knew that. I knew they probably wouldn't pick me. And I couldn't blame them, really. I had no particular ties to any of them beyond her. But I didn't want to end up with no friends.

It was shallow, selfish reason to not want to lose someone. But I decided to allow myself to be shallow and selfish. If only for a little while.

She was there before me, waiting at one of the booths by the coffee shop. She was braiding tiny bunches of her impossibly long, red hair with her also impossibly long fingers. I knew her well enough to know that she only did that when she was nervous. I sucked in a huge breath and held it in my lungs, hoping the air would somehow keep my heart from sinking. No such luck.

I sat across from Aliyah, my legs knocking against hers underneath the table. Over the last ten days, I had forgotten how tall she was. I forgot just how many freckles covered her otherwise pale skin. I forgot the way the sunlight soaked into her hair. I forgot a lot about her. She was my friend, but she was easy to forget. I felt a tsunami of guilt wash over me as soon as the thought slid into my mind. She didn't deserve that.

"Hi," I said timidly. "How are you?"

Aliyah looked up from her hair, her hands dropping to her lap. "What?" Her voice was flat.

"I—how are you?" I repeated, unsure.

She frowned, her brow furrowing. "You ignore me—everyone—for over a week and all you have to say is 'how are you?' Are you serious?"

The words knotted up in my throat. "I—I know I—I'm sorry, Aliyah—I didn't. Zoe and I broke up. I was afraid you wouldn't want me around anymore. She was your friend first."

Aliyah rubbed her temples. "So you decided to not give anyone the choice? You didn't know we'd want nothing to do with you. You assumed. How shitty do you think we are, Anna?"

"I don't think you're—"

"I really don't want to hear it, Anna. It doesn't matter."

My breath caught in my chest. "What do you mean it doesn't matter?"

"I mean I don't think I need to be around you. Not for a while anyway. I don't need someone who can just drop me like that."

"Then why did you come?"

"To tell you. Because I still respect you."

I flinched.

"I'm sorry, Anna. But you hurt me. I don't do on again off again friendships. I don't need people in my life who don't trust me. I don't need people who can just drop me," she repeated. Her voice was cold. But I couldn't argue with her. She was right.

"I'm sorry."

"I know you are," Aliyah said. "I'll see you around." She stood, gathering her things. I stared down at my fingers, twisting and pinching the tips. She looked at me for a minute before walking away—just long enough for me to look up in hopes that she had changed her mind. Not that I deserved it.

I didn't move for a long time after she left. There was a hollow feeling festering in my stomach, but it wasn't because I was sad about Aliyah. It was because I *wasn't* sad. The girl who was arguably my closest friend had decided that she didn't want anything to do with me—and probably rightfully so—and I wasn't sad. What did that say about me? About my relationships with people? About my ability to connect?

I hadn't connected with anyone since Zoe, really. And I broke up with her. And I still couldn't give a concrete reason as to why I did.

With a heavy sigh, I folded my arms over the table and laid my head down on them. I felt like I hadn't slept in a thousand years. I wanted to call Cora and talk to her about it, but I was worried that my lips and tongue and throat would be too tired to form the necessary words. And besides, she knew this would happen. My sister wasn't the type to say 'I told you so' but I felt stupid regardless.

I felt so heavy. There was so much in me and I had nowhere to put it.

"Annabella? What's wrong? Are you okay?"

I hadn't meant to show up crying at Sophia's door, but I was doing a lot of things I hadn't intended to lately. I shook my head tearfully and she took me by the arm and pulled me inside. Once the door closed, she pulled me closer and wrapped her arms around me.

I could hear her heartbeat. And I felt a little sturdier.

Squeezing my eyes shut, I wrapped my arms around her a little tighter. Her warmth was radiating through me, soaking through our clothes and into my skin. I couldn't help but marvel at how soft and warm and expansive she was. Just radiating warmth and light. She wasn't *that* much taller than me—no more so than anyone else, anyway—but I felt like she was towering over me in that moment. I felt safe.

"Do you wanna talk about what happened?" Sophia asked, squeezing me. I could feel her breath in my hair, accompanied by an overwhelming desire for her to press her lips to my head.

Which I squashed immediately.

"Yeah, I do," I said, pulling away from her even though every muscle in my body was screaming for me to stay. I wiped my eyes with the heels of my hands. "Sorry. I'm not usually messy like this. I'm not this person. I have my shit together, you know?" I felt a knot forming in my throat.

"I know, it's okay." Sophia took my hand in hers and squeezed it. "Sit down, okay? Do you want any tea or cocoa or anything?" She was still holding my hand. I didn't notice. I didn't move towards her bed, either. I just shook my head 'no.' Sophia led me to her bed and we sat down together. "C'mere," she said, sliding her hand out of mine and scooting closer to me. She wrapped her arm around my shoulder and I felt myself melting into her side.

I could feel every point where our bodies were touching.

"Tell me what happened."

And so I did. I told her about breaking up with Zoe and how I didn't know why I did it or why I missed her but didn't love her. I told her about all "our" friends really being "her" friends. I told her about ignoring them until today. I told her about Aliyah. I told her about how I didn't even miss or care about Aliyah and how I felt terrible about that. I told her about how alone I felt.

"You're not alone, Annabella. I'm right here." She almost sounded hurt.

"No, I know that. I just mean… I don't know what I mean." I bit my lip, searching for the right words. To pinpoint exactly why there was this hollow ache in my chest. "No one needs me."

"You don't need them to."

"What?"

"You don't need anyone to need you. You are a whole person independent of that. You're…. you're complex and strong and funny… and compassionate. There's nothing missing. You don't need anyone else. Why do you think you need someone to need you? You're whole by yourself. You're all you need."

I was quiet for a long time after that. I could hear her pulse. The gentle rise and fall of her breath. The slow, hesitant start of a rainstorm outside. *You don't need anyone to need you.* I let it soak in through my pores and travel through my bloodstream. *You don't need anyone to need you.* Why had I thought that I did? I didn't. She was right. I was whole by myself.

"Thank you."

"You have nothing to thank me for."

I wrapped my arm around her torso, ignoring the fluttering in my stomach. "I do. Thank you for being here. And for knowing what to say."

"Anytime, Annabella." She rubbed her thumb on my arm slowly.

"You know you can call me Anna, right?" I asked, trying to change the subject. "I know Annabella is a bit of a mouthful."

"It is. But I like it," Sophia said. "I like the way it feels in my mouth. Would you rather I called you Anna, though?" she asked, doubt creeping into her voice.

"No! Its fine, I don't mind. I just didn't know if you knew you could. I mean, I'm not weird about using nicknames with people I only recently met, but I know a lot of other people are. I was just saying. You can call me whatever you want." I felt this weird sense of joy at the fact that she wanted to keep calling me Annabella. That she liked my name. That she liked how it felt in her mouth.

"Oh really? Anything?" she asked. "George? Ingrid? Alexandra?"

I laughed. "I said anything. I don't mind, as long as it means you're still talking to me." The last word caught in my throat. Sophia shifted and I felt my body light up in the new places we were touching.

And it made me a little nauseous.

"Do you feel any better?" Sophia asked after a minute or two of quiet.

"Yeah, I do. Thanks," I said. "Sorry for showing up like this." I wiped my eyes. "And for crying all over you," I added, eyeing the wet patch on her shirt.

Sophia laughed softly. "Don't be sorry. I'm glad you came over. You can cry on me any time you need to." Her thumb was sliding back and forth on the bare skin of my arm. I felt so *warm*. So *safe*.

I woke up to the sound of Sophia's door opening. The setting sun lit up the room with fiery oranges and yellows that didn't quite match the chill I felt on my face. There was a heavy blanket draped over me—as well as one of Sophia's arms. Her fingers were tracing shapes on my hand. My head was resting on her lap. I closed my eyes again.

"Hey, Emma," she said quietly.

"Is that Annabella?" Emma asked, matching Sophia's tone.

"Yeah. She was upset earlier and came to talk. She fell asleep like two hours ago. I didn't have the heart to wake her up." Sophia laughed a little. "She had a shit day. She needed to sleep." I felt her shift under me and I considered telling her I was awake now, but my voice didn't seem to want to work.

Emma laughed, too. "So you've just been sitting there for the last two hours with her asleep on you?" The bed across the room creaked. "How's your leg feeling?"

"Oh it fell asleep over an hour ago. But it's fine. If she's not up soon, I'll wake her." She moved her arm slightly, so her fingers were no longer touching my hand. I felt the absence almost immediately. "How was your day?"

"Eh, nothing special. Killed my astronomy exam, I think. Got lunch with Allison and Elise. You're still coming tomorrow night, right?"

"I think so," Sophia said. "I think Annabella wants to come, too. If that's okay with them. I didn't think to ask."

"I'm sure it's fine, Soph. It's a party. You don't really need a formal invitation," Emma said. "Why'd she come to you to talk anyway? You guys literally just met. Doesn't she have a huge group of friends? I've literally never seen her on her own."

Sophia sighed. "They were her ex's friends, I guess." I felt a knot tying itself up in my throat. "I keep forgetting that we just met, to be honest. I feel like I've known her forever. Do you ever feel like that? Do you ever just... connect with someone like that?" Now there was a different kind of knot.

Emma was quiet for a minute before replying. "Once, but not really any other time. With this kid Elijah that I met back home over winter break. But I haven't heard from him since then." I wondered what happened with him. Why she sounded sad when she said his name.

"I don't know. It's weird but it's nice. She's nice. I like being around her." Sophia's voice dropped, even quieter than she was before. But I felt her words reverberating in my skull for a long time after she said them.

eight

sophia jane kalvak
March 21

There were a lot more people at Allison and Elise's house than Emma had let me believe there would be. When I arrived with Annabella (Emma had gotten there earlier with Jarred), the place was *packed*. I didn't recognize about 70% of the faces, either. I hated how anxious I always got at these things. I didn't know why I kept going to them. There was some part of me that hoped that, if I did, I'd eventually like them. I'd become more... sociable, or something.

It never really worked out that way.

Almost immediately after arriving, I took the water bottle of vodka that we were sharing out of Annabella's bag and took a disgustingly large gulp of it. It burned going down and I had to suppress a tiny shudder. I passed the bottle off to Annabella and watched her face contort once the booze hit her lips.

"I'm awful at shots," she laughed. "I hold it in my mouth. I can't just swallow it."

"Oh god, that's the worst. We should've gotten something less… aggressive."

"Aggressive?" she laughed again. "It's fine, don't worry about it." She took another swig, this time barely making a face. "See?" She winked at me. I was suddenly very conscious of my hands and the fact that I didn't know what to do with them. I took the bottle back from her and matched her shot.

"I'm not worried if you're not worried." I was already feeling warmer. Safer.

"Good," Annabella said with a smile. Something in me stirred uneasily.

There was a band playing in the basement of the house. Some local group I'd seen at a couple parties and liked but never pursued outside of sweaty basements and crowded garages. I couldn't remember if they were the band Emma liked or not. I looked around the basement to try to pick out her face amongst the crowd, but I couldn't.

Annabella took my hand and led me towards the front of the crowd, stationing us a couple steps away from the bassist. Did she know the band or was the atmosphere getting her pumped? She started dancing and I felt hyperaware of the space I was taking up.

Dancing always made me uncomfortable. I took another shot and offered her the bottle. She shook her head. Despite my better judgment, I took a fourth and put the bottle back in her bag. She took my hand again and started dancing with me. I tried my best to feel the liquor in my veins and stop being so self-conscious.

Two songs later, the band started playing one of the few songs of theirs that I knew the words to. My face was warm and Annabella looked so happy and so beautiful—so I took her hands and danced with her.

The band finished playing and people started to file out of the basement, but Annabella and I stayed behind with a couple friends of friends. Our fingers were still intertwined and I wondered if she noticed or if it was just inertia keeping her holding on to me. She squeezed my hand, as if to answer my unspoken question, and something inside of me lurched.

A white boy with long blonde dreads and watery eyes walked over to us, holding a handle of whiskey in his loose fingers. He was sporting an ever so classy *Live Free or Die* t-shirt (what was *with* people in this state?) and a big, idiotic smile on his face.

"Hey ladies," he slurred, lifting the handle to his lips. "Nice set, right?" A bit of whiskey dribbled out of his mouth and onto the collar of his shirt. I stifled a laugh.

"Yeah, it was rad," Annabella said. "You come to these parties often? I don't think I've seen you before."

The guy frowned. "What? Yeah. I'm always here. Are *you?*"

"Always. But I've never noticed you before." She smirked. There was a teasing lilt in her voice. She could tell it was bothering him and she loved it. I bit my lip to keep from laughing.

"Well I've never seen *you* either."

Annabella shrugged. "Oh well. Well it was… nice talking to you, I guess." She turned to walk away.

"Hey—wait. You guys want a shot?" Annabella and I exchanged a glance. "It's good whiskey."

Annabella turned around again, pulling me with her. "Sure, why not." She took the handle from him and took a long gulp of whiskey, then handed it to me. I did the same and handed it back to him.

"So do you ladies—" the boy started, but Annabella was already leading me away, back up the stairs. I looked down to catch the boy's jaw drop and his eyes narrow.

Annabella nudged my arm, laughing. "Never buy your own booze, Soph. It's too easy to get it for free."

My stomach started to crawl again, so I took another shot.

We found Emma about twenty minutes later, sitting in the living room with Jarred and Elise playing Kings. They motioned for us to come join them, so we sat on the adjacent couch. Elise, who was more than a little drunk, gave us both beers and big bear hugs.

"How are you guys?" Emma asked. She was completely wrapped around Jarred. It made me more than a little bit nauseous.

Annabella glanced at me as if to confer. "Good! That band was really rad tonight."

Emma grinned. "Yeah, I love them. Hands down the best local band."

"Oh definitely," Annabella agreed. She slid her hand out of mine to pull the water bottle out of her backpack and take another shot. She handed me the bottle and I finished it off, setting it down on the table in front of me. "I always love seeing them."

"I'm so glad you came, Sophia!" Elise told me, leaning forward and taking both of my hands in hers. "I feel like I never see you anymore! Why don't we talk more? We should hang out!"

Emma laughed. "Elise, honey, calm down. You see Sophia all the time." She stood up and glanced at me. "I'm gonna get her some water, I'll be right back." She ruffled my hair as she walked past me. Annabella laughed and fixed it for me. I was hyperaware of every point on my scalp, every strand of hair, every cell that her fingers touched.

My head was swimming. I was just drunk.

I turned to look at her and immediately felt so overwhelmed. She was so, so beautiful. There was no getting around it. Annabella Avery was the most beautiful girl I had ever seen in my entire life. She was stunning. She was ethereal. She was radiant.

The crawling in my stomach moved up to my throat and out of my mouth. "You are *gorgeous*."

Annabella's eyes widened and a smile cracked her lips. "Thanks, Soph. So are you." I felt her fingers graze the side of my thigh.

I had this feeling in my chest that I couldn't explain. This bubbling crawling knotted suffocating feeling that I had to kiss her and if I didn't the world would surely end and I couldn't *possibly* be responsible for that, could I? I took her face in my hands and pulled her close to me and kissed her and everything inside of me melted away until the exact second she started kissing me back and the room fell silent and my heart stopped and subsequently kick started into overdrive and I was on *fire*. Everything was.

I don't know how long the kiss lasted; it felt too short and infinite all at the same time. Something inside of me woke up. Sprung to life. The spiders crawled out of my ears and mouth and nose and out of the house all together. A wave of warmth replaced them. I felt like light was pouring out of my every pore, every orifice. I couldn't stop smiling.

I also couldn't look at her without wanting to kiss her again.

Emma came back in the room almost immediately after we broke apart. If she saw anything, she didn't let on. Neither did Jarred. Or Elise. Or anyone, for that matter. I wondered if I had even kissed Annabella or if I had just imagined it. Surely people several counties over must have felt the earth shift the moment our lips touched. How could everyone just be going on like it hadn't happened?

I felt like a different person. Did she?

It was like having my first kiss all over again. I felt older and more certain and was riding on some sort of high. And at the same time, I was ten years old and wanted to go home and write in my diary about this amazing person I just kissed and how they lit up every single atom in my body.

This amazing *girl*.

This beautiful *girl*.

I thought about every boy I had ever kissed, every boy I had ever let touch me or hold me or even look at me and I wondered how I could have been so stupid to waste that time kissing them or touching them or looking at them when I could have been kissing girls. When I could have been kissing Annabella.

It made so much sense. It was overwhelmingly obvious. What was I thinking?

Annabella slid her hand into mine and I felt this overpowering sense of intimacy. Just the feeling of her fingers intertwining with mine was more powerful than any kiss from any boy I'd ever known.

I looked around the room and saw everyone going about their lives completely oblivious to the fact that mine had just shifted. My gaze drifted from face to face before landing on Annabella's. I desperately wanted to know what she was thinking. If she felt what I did or if it was just another kiss to her.

It couldn't be, right?

We left the party shortly after, even though we had only been there for less than two hours. Emma and Jarred stayed behind, so it was just the two of us walking home. Our arms were linked and Annabella was clinging to me. She was cold, she said. I couldn't feel anything but her warmth.

I wanted to talk to her but there was a disconnect between my mind and my mouth. The wires somewhere had been snipped and the words in my brain couldn't find their way to my tongue. I opened my mouth and nothing came out. I wanted her to say something. To remind me what the English language sounded like so maybe I could regain mastery of it. I wanted her to talk first so I wouldn't embarrass myself. So I wouldn't say too much.

I was so happy but so afraid.

I wanted to kiss her again. And somehow that thought made it through the jumbled wires between my brain and my mouth and slipped out. Annabella stopped walking and turned her face up towards me.

I kissed her again and lit up once more. She tasted like peaches and laughter and I remember thinking that peaches were my new favorite fruit. She giggled between kisses and I felt myself melting into the pavement. Her laughter burst like carbonation in my mouth, fizzy and sweet. I kissed her again, amazed and in awe of how soft she was. How kissing her made me feel drunker than any liquor I'd ever drank. How I never wanted to stop. How even though we clung to each other, she still wasn't close enough.

Annabella. Annabella. Annabella.

I'd said before that I liked the way her name felt in my mouth. That didn't compare to how her mouth felt on mine. Nothing did.

I felt like I was awake for the first time in my entire life.

I walked her home, even though that involved walking past my dorm and she insisted that I didn't have to. I told her that it was because she'd walked me home last time we were at a party. In all honesty, I just wanted the extra minutes with her.

"I had a really great time tonight. Thanks for inviting me, Soph," Annabella told me as we walked into the lobby of her building. She was rocking back and forth on her heels, hands shoved in her front pockets.

"Thanks for coming! I had a good time, too," I said awkwardly, chewing on my lip. I tried to make eye contact with her, I really did, but my gaze kept slipping down to her lips.

"We should get breakfast tomorrow morning before we leave. If you have time, I mean," she said.

"Yeah, that sounds great. Let's aim for ten? My mom's gonna be here at noon I think."

"Okay."

"Okay."

Neither of us moved.

"Well... goodnight..." I said. Annabella held her arms out for a hug, which I gladly accepted. We stood there for what felt like two lifetimes, until she stood on her tiptoes to kiss me again. All the tension and anticipation in my body melted away. The hallway melted away. I felt like it was just the two of us, floating, suspended in air.

Nothing mattered but her lips on mine.

My mouth was tingling when I left, atoms buzzing from where she'd touched me. I caught myself continuously touching them on the walk home, tracing their shape, wondering if they looked different now. Amazed that I could feel so much on such a small area of my body. Amazed that kissing could actually be that enjoyable. Amazed that a girl as beautiful as Annabella could want to kiss me.

Just amazed, period.

My heart was pounding so hard, even after I'd already gotten home and into bed. I felt like it might give out at any minute. I was so conscious of every part of my body and my face where she had touched me, like her fingertips had left lasting indents on my skin. I was so, so warm. Everywhere. Every molecule in my body was trying its damnedest to pull me back towards her, like we were magnets.

Did she feel it? Did she feel even a fraction of what I was feeling?

When Emma came home about an hour later, I was still lying awake agonizing about it. Dying to ask her. To touch her. To hold her and taste her and feel my hands in her hair. My skin ached just thinking about it.

I wanted to pour my heart out to Emma and ask her what she thought, but when she called my name softly, I didn't respond.

nine

annabella morgan avery
March 22

There was a festival of sorts on the quad the next day. Clubs lined the perimeter with their tables and their free merch and food and email signup sheets. At the far end, a stage was set up for the local bands they'd booked. The grass in between was overflowing with students and townies alike.

The air was fresh and warm. Like spring had finally decided to show up.

Sophia and I had plans to get breakfast - something I was excessively anxious about - but the weather was too nice to not appreciate. I pulled my phone from my back pocket and texted her, asking if she wanted to check out the festival and mooch off of the free food instead. Part of me hoped that the bands would be too loud and we wouldn't be able to talk about the night before.

I didn't want to lose her. Not over something as dumb and trivial as a kiss.

Why did I kiss her?

She was straight. What was I thinking?

She texted me back almost immediately, agreeing to meet me on the quad.

I put my phone back in my pocket and sat down in the grass. I tried to ignore the growing knot in my stomach, leaning back to soak in the sun on my face instead. I knew it wasn't worth worrying about - worrying wasn't going to change whatever happened. I was making myself sick for nothing. I knew that. But that didn't untangle the knots in my gut.

A band I was vaguely familiar with - they played at some of the parties I went to - was onstage now. They were playing the one song of theirs that I knew all the words to. Which helped. I sang along under my breath while I waited for her—focusing intensely on the words instead of her face.

Or her lips.

God forbid.

Her lips.

Jesus Christ. *I need to be doused with cold water or something.* I almost laughed at the thought.

"Annabella?" The knot jumped to my throat. "I didn't think I'd find you so easily," Sophia said, sitting down beside me. Our knees touched. "It's not as busy as I thought it'd be."

"They just started playing. People will probably come soon."

"Yeah. Probably." She looked up at the band. I couldn't tell if I was feeling the bass in my chest or if it was just my heartbeat. "Is this the band that was playing at that party? The one we met at?"

"Oh - yeah, I think so. They're pretty good. I don't know a lot of their stuff though, I just hear it at parties."

"Emma really likes them. She burned me a CD but I haven't gotten around to listening to it yet."

"Oh. Cool." Definitely my heartbeat.

After what felt like a lifetime, I finally worked up the guts to look at her, but her eyes were still on the band. I didn't want to stare at her but I couldn't help it. She was so beautiful. Every time I pulled my gaze away I found it drifting back. Every sensory nerve in my body was redirected to the point on my knee where we were touching.

I knew I needed to stop. To get over this crush and just be her friend. It was pointless—she was straight. She was straight. I was wasting my time and energy. And I was probably just... lonely. It didn't mean anything. It didn't mean anything. It didn't mean anything. But I couldn't not feel the small fire that was starting on our knees. As much as I wanted to.

I was exhausting myself and I hadn't even managed to talk to her yet.

There was a lull between songs as the guitarist swapped out guitars - he broke a string or something. Sophia turned away from the band to look back at me. And caught me staring at her.

Shit.

"What's up?" she asked coolly. Maybe I didn't need to bring it up. Maybe it was fine. Maybe it didn't mean anything to her.

"Nothing. I just," I sighed. "Sorry about last night, dude."

"Sorry for what?" She sounded genuinely confused. Did she not remember?

I bit my lip. I couldn't not tell her now. Even if she didn't remember - I brought it up. "For kissing you. I didn't mean anything by it. I was just really drunk and I - are you laughing?"

Sophia covered her mouth for a second, stifling the last couple giggles. "Is that what you're so stiff about? Annabella, I kissed you. I don't know what you're apologizing for."

The wave of relief that washed over me was impossibly strong. And then what she actually said hit me and uncertainty swept over me. "You did?"

"Yeah, I did," Sophia said shyly. "The first two times anyway. The third time was you."

"Why?" I asked before I could stop myself. I had to know if it meant anything. I tried telling myself that it didn't matter—I had literally *just* gotten out of a relationship and wasn't ready for anything else anyway. But I was so drawn to her. I was so into her. It felt so good to acknowledge that. To not lie to myself. To not shove my feelings down and pretend they didn't exist.

To entertain the idea that maybe she was into me, too.

Sophia looked away. "I don't know. I wanted to." She seemed so confident just a minute ago. What changed?

"Why, though?" I asked again, swallowing my anxieties. "Do you always kiss girls when you're drunk, or…?" I felt so stupid. I was never really one to fumble my words or not know what to say, but I was so nervous. I didn't want to say the wrong thing. I didn't want to imply something that wasn't true.

I didn't want her to know how I was feeling if she didn't feel the same.

She's straight.

Sophia laughed, but she sounded nervous. "No, I don't. That was a first." She chewed on her lip. I felt mildly nauseous. And yet, I wanted to kiss her again. She turned back to me, brow furrowed. "I really like you, Annabella. I like how I feel around you. I like who I am around you."

My heart froze mid-beat for what felt like an hour before restarting. I swear everyone on the quad could feel it's pounding after that. "Really?"

Sophia nodded and my mouth ran dry. I opened my mouth to try to tell her I felt the same but the words wouldn't come out. They were stuck somewhere between my mouth and my chest, looming in the back of my throat. I was choking on them.

I liked her so much. Too much. I didn't want to ruin things by going too quickly. I didn't want to lose her as a friend by jumping into a relationship so soon after breaking my own heart with Zoe.

"It's okay if you don't feel the same. I still want to be friends. I just. I don't know. I'm sorry I said anything." Sophia looked away from me, down at her hands. She was twisting and tugging on her own fingers.

My heart jumped into my throat. "No, it's not that, I swear. I feel the same about you. I just. I just broke up with Zoe. I'm not really… ready, I guess. For us to be anything but friends." I paused. "I feel like such an ass, I shouldn't have pushed you to tell me. I'm sorry. I care about you a lot though, dude, and I really don't want to fuck this up."

Sophia was quiet. I felt my heartbeat in every cell in my body, pounding away. Shaking the ground underneath me. Could she feel it? "Okay. I understand. I don't want you to do anything you're not ready for. I'm probably not ready either. This is… unexpected to say the least." She laughed. That was a good sign, right? "I'm not the type to fall for someone so quickly. And the whole girl thing was a surprise," she laughed again. "I want us to be friends either way. Anything else is just… a bonus."

I smiled and took her hand, squeezing it tightly. "Thanks for being so understanding. And sorry for being lame about this."

She squeezed my hand back. "You're not being lame. There's no need to jump into anything. You're fine. We're fine."

"I'm glad."

We laid in the grass talking about nothing for another two hours before her mom arrived to pick her up. When she left, I wrapped my arms around her tightly and tried not to think about kissing her. I was the one who wanted to keep things platonic for now. I had no right thinking about her lips. I had no right wanting her. I was the one who wasn't ready.

She kissed the top of my head before letting go of me and I felt like I was going to explode. But I made an effort to show no outward distress; I simply smiled and waved and wished her a good spring break.

I felt her absence the second she walked away.

Cut it out.

Cora and I left shortly after Sophia did. We spend the majority of the car ride in unusual silence. Usually the two of us never shut up when we were together, but I was feeling so sick and conflicted that I couldn't make myself talk. What was wrong with me? Why could I never commit to my decisions? Why could I never understand them? Why did I always feel so… disconnected from the things I chose to do?

I didn't understand why I was suddenly feeling so reserved about Sophia just like I didn't understand why I decided to break up with Zoe. It was like my heart was making its own decisions and not informing my brain of the reasons why.

"Okay, what's the problem, Anna?" Cora asked about fifteen minutes into our trip.

"What problem?"

"Whatever problem you're having. I presume it's about Zoe or something. But you're never quiet like this unless you have a problem. So spill. We've still got another half hour of driving to do, so you can either get it all out now or we can talk at home where Moms can hear," Cora said matter-of-factly.

I sighed. "It's not about Zoe. Well, I guess it kind of is. But it's also about this other girl. Sophia Kalvak."

"What happened?"

"I don't know. I like her." Something about saying it felt good. Better than I expected. I felt the weight of the words in my mouth and smiled. And then immediately chastised myself for it. I liked her. But maybe that wasn't the best thing for me right now.

God, nothing could ever be simple. I never let it be simple. What was wrong with me?

"Is she why you broke up with Zoe?"

I shook my head. If anyone else had asked me that, I would have been so offended. "I didn't even know her then."

"So what's the problem? She doesn't like you back?" Cora didn't get it. But then, neither did I.

"No, she does."

"Again… where's the problem? The timing? Cuz you know there's never a good time for this kind of thing to happen. If you guys like each other you should go for it." I was starting to get a headache. *She's missing the point,* I thought. And then; *am I even making a point?*

I shook my head again. "It's not that simple. I still don't know what went wrong with Zoe and me. And I really like this girl, Char. I don't want to mess up. What if what wrong with me and Zoe goes wrong with me and Soph? I don't want to risk it." I sighed. I knew it was easier than I was making it out to be, but I was tangling myself up in manufactured worries. I knew what happened with Zoe and me—whatever it was—wouldn't happen with me and Sophia. Because Sophia was different from Zoe. And I was different when I was with her.

I like who I am around you.

"Things go wrong in life, kid. You can't sit around not doing anything because of all the ways it might go wrong. You'll miss out on the ways it could go right," Cora told me. "She's not Zoe. Zoe was no good for you, dude, she was controlling as fuck. You dodged a bullet there. If it's the Sophia I'm thinking of, I've heard only good things about her. She's friends with Emma Braxton, right?" I nodded. "Then from what I know of her, she's the polar opposite of Zoe. But if you guys both like each other, things could go bad either way. Being friends with someone you have a crush on isn't easy, dude. Might as well give it a shot."

I took a deep breath, letting my lungs expand fully. I held it in for a long time before finally letting it out. "I guess…"

"What's the worst that could happen?" my sister asked.

God, what *was* the worst that could happen?

"We break up and become strangers again."

"You've known this girl for what, two weeks? You were fine without her then, you'd be fine without her after. Now what's the best case scenario?"

I frowned. "I don't know? We grow old together and have 2.5 kids and big yard with a white picket fence," I said sarcastically. "Isn't that the best case scenario for any relationship?"

Cora laughed. "Okay, sure. So what's the best and worst case scenario of you guys just staying friends?"

"We stay friends forever or we become strangers again."

"So the worst case scenarios are the same, then. Which best case scenario sounds better to you?" my sister asked.

I sighed. "I don't want to talk about this anymore."

"You know I'm right."

She was. Of course she was. "Be quiet."

ten

sophia jane kalvak
March 22

My mother and I didn't talk. Not just during
the car ride home. We just didn't talk. Ever, really.
She was uptight and reserved and I was always too
anxious to break her carefully crafted silence. When
we talked, it was in brief matter-of-fact statements.
Your grandmother's birthday is next week. I made
lasagna for dinner. Your uncle finally sent you a
birthday card, make sure you call him. Nothing that
opened a discussion. Nothing I could say anything
but "okay" or "yes" or "I know" to.

And it was fine, really, except for the fact
that I felt like my entire life had changed the night
before. I'd never felt this overpowering desire to
talk to my mother about anything before, but I did
now.

But suddenly, like I was hit with a ton of
bricks, I remembered the way I had heard her and
her church friends hiss and spit the word

homosexual. I bit my tongue, feeling the rosy pink bubble I was floating on suddenly just… *pop*!

I couldn't stop thinking about Annabella for the rest of the day. I wanted to pretend that I was struggling with it, that I was bad or gross or wrong. That I was wrong. That I was drunk and I kissed her and so what? Straight girls kiss each other all the time when they're drunk, right? I wanted to pretend that I thought I was wrong.

But I couldn't.

I couldn't pretend that kissing her meant nothing. I couldn't pretend that it hadn't lit up all the darkest parts of me. I couldn't pretend that it was unlike any kiss I had ever experienced before. I couldn't pretend that I didn't love the way she tasted and the way she felt in my arms and the way she laughed in between kisses. I couldn't. I couldn't.

I never wanted to talk to my mom before. I was always… well, not comfortable, but at the very least *okay with* our silence. With the way we rarely spoke. It gave us less time to disagree. Not that I ever dared to voice my dissent.

It was early still, barely seven pm, but I crawled into bed and pulled the blankets up to my chin anyway. I wanted to sleep so I wouldn't have to worry anymore. I would talk to her tomorrow, maybe. If I had the guts.

She's my mom. She has to still love me.

The next morning came far too quickly. My mother woke me up by turning all the lights on in my room and pulling my blanket away from my face. "Sophia, get up. It's time for church." I tried to remember if her voice was always so quiet and forceful. Living away from her always made me forget. I'd convince myself that I turned her into a caricature of a human being in my head. But every time I came home, I was struck by how lifelike my memory was. I was always right in my memory of her mannerisms, I just never trusted myself to be for some reason.

"Okay. I'll be down in a second. Sorry." For what I was apologizing for I had no idea, but it always seemed to be the appropriate thing to do when she spoke to me. Apologize. Make myself smaller. More obedient. Less... everything. My mother shrunk me down to the size of a three year old every time I saw her again.

Maybe that wasn't fair of me to think. She did love me. I knew that. There was just a disconnect in the way I knew and the way I felt.

It didn't usually bother me, but there was a dark pit opening up in my stomach.

Church was... church. I wore some stuffy 'nice' clothes that I hated, listened to some old guy preach about Jesus and the apostles, shook hands with old white people, and put cardboard in my mouth. Afterwards, in the reception hall, people my mother was friends with asked me if I liked school and if I still went to church up there. I told them I loved it and of course I did.

Tiny pieces of me felt like they were dying and flaking off, congregating with the dust on the old wooden floors. I sipped my apple juice and wondered how long it would take for my entire body to go that way.

We always stayed at these things way too long.

In the car on the way home, I swallowed the tumor in my throat and fumbled for the words I was looking for.

"Do you believe what they say at church? Like, all of it?" I asked, staring directly ahead. I could see every piece of dirt, every watermark, every speck of pollen on the windshield. I focused so hard on a broken piece of leaf that couldn't see the road ahead of us.

"Yes."

I bit down on the inside of my lip, almost wanting to draw blood. "Even like, the stuff from the Old Testament? Like before Jesus. Like. Leviticus and all that?"

"What are you fishing for, Sophia? You need to be more direct."

I unclenched my jaw, feeling it pop somewhere. "I know. I'm sorry. I just mean. I have this friend who's, you know... gay. Do you believe that she's going to Hell?"

"*Thou shalt not lie with mankind, as with womankind: it is abomination.*"

"I know what the Bible says, Mom, I'm asking what *you* think." I felt like all the air had been punched out of my lungs. "Do you believe that?"

"Yes."

I could feel my heartbeat in my throat, choking me. "But she's like, a really good person, you know? Do you think God would really send her to Hell over that one thing? She isn't... she isn't hurting anyone, Mom." *Do not cry, do not cry, do not cry, do not cry.*

I wanted to throw up.

"A sin is a sin, Sophia. She's hurting her soul. What she's doing is wrong, and she can only find healing and peace through penance and forgiveness from God."

"But what does she need to forgive her for?"

"For turning away from him and embracing sin. Homosexuality is a sin, Sophia, you know that. Just as adultery and blasphemy and false idol worship are sins." My mother's voice was sharp, exact. It felt like a scalpel ripping through my stomach.

"But those are *choices*. She didn't chose this. God just... made her that way."

My mother snorted. "God doesn't make mistakes. Men are meant to be with women and vice versa. God created Adam and Eve as two parts of one whole. If we were meant to be *homosexual*, don't you think He would have started us off that way?" I could see her shake her head out of the corner of my eye. "Besides, we are all born with the capacity to do sin. It is not homosexual desire that's the sin, it's the act. I know many people who struggle with homosexuality who remain celibate. God does not condemn them."

"*Mistakes*? Mom, she's not a—"

"I don't want you hanging out with this girl anymore, Sophia. It's clear that she's driving you away from God. Does your school have a Faith Club or something? Maybe you could make some friends there, instead."

God, I didn't want to say it. I wanted to back out. I wanted to drop the conversation. But I couldn't. "I can't just stop hanging out with her, Mom…"

"I know it's hard but you can't help her, only God can. Did you hear what I said about the Faith Club?"

There was something heavy and jagged lodged in my throat. I tried to cough it out to no avail. So instead, I let the words spill out: "Mom, I can't stop hanging out with myself."

"What?" The temperature in the car dropped several thousand degrees. I swore I could see my breath.

"I can't stop hanging out with her. It's me." I spit out the words so quickly that for a millisecond, I wasn't even sure I had said them. I wasn't sure I hadn't imagined it.

We stopped short and I jerked forward, the seatbelt catching me in the throat. "Get out of the car, Sophia."

"What?" Tears sprung into my eyes.

"You heard me. Get out of the car. Now."

"But Mom, I—"

"Out."

I unbuckled my seatbelt with numb, broken fingers, sobs wracking my chest. I couldn't even tell what I was saying, my words were so muffled by my tears. I stepped out of the car and stood on the sidewalk, hands limp by my side. The noises coming from my chest were animalistic. Inhuman and broken.

My mother shut the car door and drove away.

I sat on the side of the road crying for the better part of an hour, completely wrecked and unsure of what to do. When I finally stopped crying, I numbly pulled my phone out of my back pocket. I didn't expect any texts or calls from my mom, but part of me hoped there were some.

But I guess if she felt bad she would have turned around and came back for me.

There were no missed calls. Just a good morning text from Annabella that made me a little sick.

I didn't know what else to do, so I called my nana and told her where I was. If she heard my voice break, she didn't mention it. She was good like that.

My nana lived forty minutes away, but she made it there in twenty. When I got in the passenger seat of her car she silently handed me a Dunkin Donuts cup of hot chocolate. Just holding it in my frozen hands and feeling the warmth seep into my skin made me feel better already. She took my free hand in hers and squeezed tightly before taking the wheel, but didn't say anything.

I brought the cup to my lips and let the steam kiss me for a bit before taking a sip. It somehow managed to be the perfect temperature, just like it always was when she got it for me. Somehow when I ordered my own hot chocolate it was always scalding. The warm liquid slid down my throat, washing away any leftover knots and coating it so no new ones would stick.

I caught myself wondering what my life would've been like if I had my nana for a mother instead of my mother. Somehow, I still managed to feel guilty for that.

"Do you want to talk about what happened, sweetheart?" Nana asked. I had been sitting at the dining room table for over an hour, just staring at my hands. The tears came and went, but I was too exhausted to cry hard anymore. I couldn't even lift my hands to wipe them away. I felt so weak and exhausted and hurt. My muscles ached.

She placed another mug of hot chocolate in front of me, this time homemade. I didn't have the energy to make my arms move. It went cold in front of me.

After a long time, I shrugged. "She made me get out of the car and left." My mouth felt like sandpaper. If my muscles weren't so exhausted, I might have vomited. There was bile somewhere, working its way up, but my body didn't have the strength left in it to help it.

"Who is she? Not your mother?"

I nodded.

"Why on earth would she do that, dear?" She sat down across from me, folding her thin, wrinkled hands in front of her. "Did you get into an argument? That's very unlike you, Sophia."

I swallowed. "I guess we did, yeah. I don't know. I can stay here though, right?" I felt fresh tears spring to my eyes. I knew what she would say, of course, but I wanted her to say it before I told her what we fought over. I wanted her to tell me I could stay before she knew. So she couldn't take it back afterwards.

I was so afraid shew as going to take it back afterwards.

My nana smiled, and I almost felt warm. "Sophia Jane Kalvak, you know you never need to ask me that. You're always welcome here. Do you want to tell me what you and your mother fought about? I'm sure it was just a little spat. She's always been tightly wound, honey. She'll get over it."

I took a deep breath, filling my lungs to capacity. "I said... I told her..." The water in my eyes was drowning me. I blinked the tears away, pretending I didn't notice them sliding down my cheeks and plopping on the table in front of me. "I think I'm a lesbian, Nana."

"And she kicked you out for *that*?" I had seen my nana get angry exactly twice in my life. Once when my uncle told her that he was moving to Connecticut and again when she got in a fight with my mother about politics. Neither of those compared to how angry she looked right now.

I nodded, terrified.

I shouldn't have told her.

"Because of her goddamn bible, I'm assuming?" Nana rubbed her temples. "*But if anyone does not provide for his own, and especially for those of his household, he has denied the faith and is worse than an unbeliever,"* she quoted. "Guess she forgot about that one, huh?" She walked over to me and wrapped her arms around me tightly. "I'm sorry, baby." She kissed me forehead. "I love you endlessly. And your mom does, too. She'll remember that sooner or later. But until then, you always have a place with me."

"Thank you, Nana. I love you, too."

She sat down in the chair next to me, hands clasped tightly around mine. "Now, I presume you've met a girl?" she asked, smiling.

I laughed, wiping my tears away on my sleeve. "Yeah. I did." I smiled. I was starting to feel warm again. I was thawing.

She squeezed my hand. "Tell me about her. I want to make sure she's good enough for my grandbaby."

I spent the next half hour stumbling through a useless description of Annabella. I told her how beautiful she was. How long and curly and soft her hair was. How mesmerizing her eyes were. How soft her skin was. I told her how we could talk about anything. God, love, death, ghosts, aliens… anything. I told her how she made me feel like springtime. How I felt flowers on my skin when we touched or just when we were together. How I had never felt like that about anyone before. How I didn't even think I *could* feel like that about anyone.

"It sounds like you've got it bad, baby girl," Nana said when I finally stopped. She put her hand on my knee. "She sounds great."

"She is great."
"I'm happy for you."
I was happy for me, too.

eleven

annabella morgan avery
March 25

It was always noisy at my house. With the combined noise of me and my two sisters, the dogs, my Moms, and the constant background noise of someone's TV or someone's radio, it was hard to find a moment of silence. Normally I didn't mind the noise. I grew up with it. I was used to it. I found the absence of noise more distracting than the presence. But it was getting to me this week. It was boring holes in my skull and causing everything I was trying to work through to leak out. It was driving me *insane*.

So I took Ma's keys off of the rack and left, hoping that she and Mom planned on carpooling today. If not, she could take Char's car. I wasn't too concerned.

It felt immediately therapeutic to be driving down the familiar back roads of my town. Similar to the one time I had a panic attack and Mom gave me

Xanax for it. The relief came in waves, slowly tugging the tension and worry from each of my limbs individually and methodically. Something vaguely similar to taking off tight clothes after a long day. Like taking off the blood pressure cuff. Expansion. Returning to normal. Increased blood flow. *Something.*

I felt like I could breathe properly again. My headache cleared. I could think.

I drove in silence for a while, listening to Ma's old car sputtering and clunking on the cracked, rocky pavement. When I couldn't stand that anymore, I turned on the radio and started listening to whatever cd it was Ma had in there. I couldn't help but smile when I recognized it as the mix I made for her before I left for my first year of college. She always listened to it when she missed me.

I wondered how long the cd had been in there. How long she'd missed me for.

I found myself driving to my old high school, were Liliana was currently in class. Running on autopilot, I pulled up to the front doors, turned off the car, and went inside. I wasn't sure if I had privileges to dismiss my baby sister from school, but I was about to find out. I'd had my fill of being alone. And I hadn't seen her once since getting home Saturday afternoon.

The secretary was the same grumpy, unfriendly woman who was there during my four years. I don't know why I expected anything differently—it wasn't like schools regularly cycled through different secretaries. But something in me had just assumed that once I left that things would change. If I wasn't going there then it only stood to reason that none of the regular fixtures in my High School Experience would remain. Which was stupid in some sort of cosmic narcissistic way, I guess.

"Hi, I'm here to dismiss Liliana Avery. I'm her sister. Annabella," I told the secretary, who I was fairly certain didn't remember me. She held out her hand for my ID, which I quickly presented. She glanced at it briefly and shooed me, picking up the phone. I sat down on one of the folding chairs across the hall and waited.

Ma would probably be mad at me for dismissing her, but Mom would calm her down. The day was nearly over, anyway. It was almost 12:30. She probably only had a class and a half left.

I mean, she didn't even really have to tell them. The school wouldn't call, I was authorized.

Liliana came walking down the hall a few minutes later, her backpack slung over one shoulder. Her long, curly hair was dyed a bright, shocking blue. I hadn't seen her since January, but we'd talked every few days—somehow her hair change never came up.

"Hey, Lil. Nice hair," I said, standing up. "Let's go."

"Thanks. What's up? Why are you dismissing me?"

"I felt like it." I shrugged.

"Well. Alright then."

"So, what's your problem?" Lil asked once we got on the highway. She turned to face me in the passenger seat, one of her long, thin legs tucked neatly underneath herself.

"What do you mean what's my problem?" I asked, glancing at her. "I don't have a problem. Do *you* have a problem? Are you projecting, Liliana?"

My sister snorted. "Oh shut up. The only time you take me on drives to nowhere like this is when you have something on your mind. Have you talked to Char about it?"

I sighed. She wasn't wrong. "Yeah, I did."

"Is it about Zoe? It's always about a girl. What'd she do now? Do I need to beat her up for you, An?"

I shook my head. "No, it's not about Zoe. We broke up actually." I paused. "I broke up with her, I mean. Like two weeks ago. Didn't I tell you?" I pressed my foot down harder on the gas, watching the arrow on the speedometer tick past seventy five and beeline for eighty. Liliana didn't say anything. "I met this other girl. I didn't break up with Zoe because of her—I didn't even meet her until afterwards—but. I don't know. I feel really… drawn to her, I guess. Does that ever happen to you? You just meet someone and you feel so… comfortable. So safe and at ease. Like you've known each other forever."

Lil cleared her throat. "I mean, that's never happened to me before, but I kinda get what you mean, I think. We got kind of off topic in my lit class today, talking about like. Soulmates and love and all that boring shit I know you love," my little sister laughed. "But we were talking about how ancient Chinese people—I think it was them anyway—thought that people who were meant to be together were connected by this thread or something. Maybe that's why you feel drawn to her. Maybe you guys have that thread."

"I didn't say she was my *soulmate*, Lil, don't make it weird!" I laughed.

Liliana laughed, too. "No, I know you didn't. I'm just saying. A lot of cultures believe that your... your souls can know each other or something, y'know? That's all soulmate really means. None of that weird one-true-love shit. You know I don't buy that," she said. "All I'm saying is if they're right—and who fucking knows, they might be—maybe that's why. Anything's possible and all that."

I laughed. "Maybe."

"Have you told her how you felt? I'm asking as a formality, because I know your gay little heart couldn't keep it in and you already told her. What did she say?"

"Oh my *god*, Lil! You could at least *pretend* not to know how weak and pathetic I am when it comes to this shit." I tried to pretend to be offended, but I still couldn't stop laughing. "Yeah, I told her. She likes me, too."

"So what's the problem?"

"I don't know, you tell me."

She was quiet for a minute. "Well, I think your problem is that you're an idiot—wait, hear me out. You know that I love you and think the world of you. You are very smart and blah blah blah. But you are an idiot when it comes to things like this. You overthink so fast that you don't even realize you thought it, let alone overthought it. I bet that's what happened with Zoe, too. So you like this girl, right, and before you can even consciously think 'hey, I like this girl' you've already gone over every scenario in your head of what could go wrong. You've already thought the relationship out from beginning to bitter, bitter end. And sure, maybe you should trust your instincts and accept the end of the relationship you never even let yourself have, because you *are* smart. You are. But you don't account for other people very well," Liliana said.

"You think out everything *you* could do wrong. You think out every way *you* would react to the things *you* do wrong. This other girl didn't even factor into it. She was just a... a Barbie doll in your little game. You didn't think of the ways she'd react to the wrongs you'd do, like you didn't think of the wrongs she specifically would do. So your conclusion is inherently flawed."

"What does that mean?" I asked.

"It means you need to get out of your own damn head for five seconds and just *live*. Let yourself make mistakes in real time. Let her make mistakes. Let shit fall apart IRL instead of in your little subconscious dream world." Only Liliana could use text-speak in person and still sound smarter than me. "I'm not saying like, you need to date this girl or you need to get back with Zoe— god, don't get back with Zoe—but like. Step back. Pull your head out of your ass and look around. Try and see what's actually happening instead of every bad thing that *could* happen, you know?"

"Who let you get so smart, Lil?"

She laughed. "No idea, but aren't you lucky that they did?"

"You still haven't told me anything about her," Liliana said as the waitress walked away. I'd decided to treat her to her favorite restaurant I exchange for her impressive sixteen year old wisdom. "What's her name?"

"Sophia." I took a sip of my water. "Her name is Sophia."

"What does she look like?"

The water caught in my throat. "I'm shit at describing people, I won't do her justice."

"Try."

"Well. She's tall. Taller than you. She's got long black hair that's like, impossibly soft and shiny. She's got really dark brown eyes but like, the warm kind of dark, you know? She has a really cute nose. It's weird to think that a nose is cute but hers definitely is. And when she laughs it scrunches up. It's the kind of nose you just want to kiss." Liliana laughed. "Shut up."

"What else?"

"She's soft and warm. That's not really how she looks but she is. She makes you feel safe. She makes me feel safe, anyway." I didn't usually get embarrassed about this sort of thing, but I could feel heat crawling up my spine and spreading across my face. Liliana wasn't interested in this sort of thing; she was only asking because she cared about me. Which was nice, but it made it weird to talk about it with her. "She's beautiful. She's like. A goddess. I don't know," I finished awkwardly.

"How did you meet her?"

I laughed. "At a party. She was drunk and crying on the steps and I was trying to leave. And you know me, I couldn't just leave her there. So I walked her home. She was so trashed but she was talking a lot and it was really cute and she was just... interesting, I don't know. Like I said, I just feel very drawn to her. So we hung out the next day. And a bunch of times since then. And then we went to another party on Friday night and she kissed me. Like a lot," I laughed. "That wasn't really what you asked."

"It's fine, An. Have you told Moms about her?"

"Oh god, no. They'll want to meet her immediately. We're not even dating."

"Sounds like you should be."

"Shhh. Let's talk about you now. How have you been? Have you fallen madly in love yet? Gotten a job? Overthrown capitalism? Seen a dog?"

Liliana laughed. "Good, disgusting, no, working on it, and yes."

"Disgusting?"

"I'm better than that, Anna. Falling in love is for the weak—no offence."

"Ooh, some taken."

"I've got more important things to do. Like overthrowing capitalism, apparently," she laughed. "Seems like an overall waste of time. And it destroys morals, apparently, too. I mean, look at you. One little crush and you're encouraging truancy in your poor little sister, speeding down the highway, crying about *soulmates*."

"Hey, you brought up soulmates, not me," I laughed. "But yeah, I guess you're right. It rots you to the core. Learn from me, kiddo. Don't go down this path. It's terrible."

The waitress set down our orders. "Yeah, thank god I have you here to show me how wrong a person could be. My fuck up big sister. What would I do without you?" The waitress made a face and we both burst out laughing.

"I missed you," I told her. "Seriously, how have you been?"

"I missed you too, Anna. I've been good. Just a lot of the same old shit, you know. Nothing exciting. Nothing worth brining up."

"Nothing at all?"

Liliana shrugged. "Nope, not really. I'm super boring. My life is super boring and tragic. Sorry to disappoint." She swept her brilliant blue locks to one side.

I got the feeling that she was hiding something from me, which was so unlike her that I didn't even try to push it. If she didn't want to tell me, I trusted that she had a good reason for it. Trusting Liliana was usually a good choice. I would never want to inflate her ego any more by telling her, but she was usually right. Trusting her never really led me wrong before.

She was smarter than me. I'd never seriously tell her that, either.

When we got home, Liliana immediately threw me under the bus. "Annabella broke up with Zoe. She likes another girl. You should talk to her about it." I jabbed her with my elbow. "She said she really wants to talk to you two about it. She told Char and me already but apparently neither of us are smart enough."

"Liliana!" I hissed. "I told you I didn't want to tell them."

"Yeah, well. I know you're not going to listen to me without some sort of accountability. So unfortunately, Moms had to get involved." She kissed me on the cheek. "Good luck."

"I hate you," I whispered as Moms walked into the room. "You're terrible."

"I'm amazing and you love me. I'm going to go do homework now."

"What's that about Zoe?" Ma asked, sitting down at the counter. I leaned forward, resting my elbows on the counter and my head in my hands. "You two finally broke up?"

"Finally?"

Mom sat down next to Ma, sliding her hand into hers almost automatically. They were always touching somehow. Like they couldn't bear to be apart, even after all their years of being together.

Ma shrugged. "I never really liked her. Sorry if it ended poorly, but not sorry it ended."

"What'd your sister say about another girl?" Mom asked. "Who is she? What's she like?"

"Her name is Sophia," I said.

"You must be sick of talking about her by now if you already told Cora and Liliana separately. We won't push. But we'd love to meet her sometime," Mom told me, smiling warmly.

I thought that I probably should have been sick of talking about it by now, but I wasn't. I didn't think I would ever be sick of talking about Sophia. But I smiled back and let the conversation drop, because I didn't want to get their hopes up.

Liliana was a million times smarter than me and I knew she was right, but that didn't make it easy. I didn't know how to get out of my own head. I didn't even realize how deep in there I was until she pointed it out to me.

twelve

sophia jane kalvak
March 26

"Do I have to go with you?" I asked, my heart dropping into the pit in my stomach. "I really don't want to see her. And she doesn't want to see me. It would be better for you to just go get my stuff. I'll stay here and… clean or something. Please don't make me go, Nana. Please." I begged, my eyes burning.

"She's not going to say anything to you, Sophia. I want you to come with me. I won't make you, but I think you should," my nana said. "You don't need to be afraid of her, sweetheart. I'll be with you. I just need your help getting your things. She wasn't very agreeable on the phone, I doubt she got your things together like I asked her to."

I bit down on my lip. "I guess."

"You have nothing to be afraid of," Nana said, kissing my forehead. "Come on, let's go. We'll go out to eat afterwards."

The car ride to my mother's house was excruciating. Each minute that passed was absolutely agonizing. Each minute meant I was one minute closer to facing her. The woman who no longer loved me. Something in my chest shattered over and over and over, pieces crumbling off and turning to dust with each passing second. I wanted to bang my head against the window.

We stopped at Dunkin Donuts on the way and Nana bought me another hot chocolate, but I couldn't bring myself to drink it. I was too nauseous. I wanted to, but I wanted to vomit in her car even less.

Somehow, I didn't think that that would help the situation.

I had hoped that my mother wouldn't be home when we got there, but of course she was. Where else would she be?

My nana opened the door without knocking, entered without announcing herself. I could feel flames coming off of her body. I cowered in her shadow, a terrified little girl.

My mother was in the kitchen making herself lunch. I heard her fussing with dishes when we first walked in, but once she heard us she went dead silent.

I could hear my heart beat reverberating off of the plain white walls. There were massive tarantulas crawling around the walls of my stomach and up the back of my throat. A knot somewhere behind my ribs was tightening. I wanted to run back out of the house, get in my nana's car, and drive all the way back to New Hampshire and never come back. I wanted to show up at Annabella's door sobbing like she'd come to mine. I wanted her to hold me and kiss me and tell me that everything would be okay. I wanted to leave the country. I wanted to never see my mother again. I wanted my dad.

Something inside me snapped and tears sprung to my eyes.

I followed my nana to my bedroom, too afraid to walk ahead of her. The hallway walls were sliding closer to us, boxing me in. I wouldn't have minded, if only they went a little further and crushed me between them. That seemed to be a more favorable outcome to my trip home than talking to my mother.

I glanced behind me to see if she was still in the kitchen. She was. She stood over the counter with her back towards me, hands limp at her sides. I wondered why she wasn't moving. Why she wasn't doing anything. If the walls were closing in on her, too.

I wanted her to say something. My name. I'm sorry. Anything. I wanted her to talk to me and to never even look at me again all at once and it was driving bile up the back of my throat.

My nana pushed my bedroom door open with one hand, the other reaching back and holding my arm. I felt immediately steadied by her, but not quite enough to quell the seasickness I was experiencing. I took a deep breath, finding myself caught off guard by how easy it was. How the air around me was, in fact, air, and not salty sea water.

I was drowning nonetheless.

Nana shut the door behind us and looked around the room. "See, she didn't get your things together like I asked. I told you she wouldn't." She shook her head. I shivered. It was about ten thousand degrees colder in my room than it was in the hallway. "Go ahead and get your things. I'm going to go talk to Olivia."

"About what?"

Nana rolled her eyes. "The weather, Sophia. Just stay in here until I call you, alright?" she said, taking my hand and squeezing it one more time before leaving the room and closing the door behind her. I took a deep breath, the freezing air stiffening my lungs, and wondered why I always felt so out of breath lately. No matter how deeply or often I breathed, I never managed to catch my breath.

My heart was alternating between fluttering and pounding, unsure if it was a bird or a dragon.

I knew I shouldn't listen in, but somehow I found myself with my ear pressed against the door, straining to hear them down the hall. When I couldn't make anything out, me and my dragon-heart crept out of my room and edged down the hallway. They were on the other side of the kitchen now; completely out of sight but not out of earshot.

"I raised you better than this, goddammit. She's your daughter."

"I didn't raise that girl. I don't know who she is."

"She's your *daughter*, Olivia. She's the same girl she was before she told you. She's the same girl who has made you breakfast in bed every mother's day and birthday since she was five years old. The same daughter who you used to be so quick to brag about at parties. The daughter you *love*, Olivia. She's still smart and brave and loyal and honest and compassionate, just like you raised her to be."

"Homosexuality is a sin," my mother answered like a robot. There was no emotion behind her words. No conviction. No *anything*. It was like nothing my nana said registered or mattered.

"Christ, Olivia, so is kicking her out. Timothy 5:8." Nana said matter-of-factly. "Or did you forget who taught you to read the Bible? You think I don't know what it says?" Nana asked. "Leviticus is an old outdated code of morals, not something you, a twenty first century Christian, need to take into account. And she's your *daughter*."

"I don't understand it. I raised her—"

"You raised her exactly the damn way she is, Olivia! Do you think she would chose this? She's terrified of you!" I had never heard my nana yell before. "For god's sake, stop hiding behind the Bible and admit that you were wrong." I heard footsteps and a drawer opening. Pages fluttering. "Do you remember your wedding vows, Olivia?"

My mother was quiet for a very long time. "Ruth 1:16-17."

"*'Don't urge me to leave you or to turn back from you. Where you go I will go, and where you stay I will stay. Your people will be my people and your God my God. Where you die I will die, and there I will be buried. May the Lord deal with me, be it ever so severely, if anything but death separates you and me.'* Those are them, right? Who said that, Olivia?"

"Ruth."

I heard the Bible close heavily and drop down on the counter. "To whom?"

I didn't have to see my mother to know the look she was giving my nana right now. I could feel it. It chilled my bones and shattered them. "To Naomi."

"From one woman to another. And somehow, bigots like you see fit to use it to describe their marital love while demonizing the women it came from in the very next breath." There was a pause. "I'm not going to tell you what to believe, Olivia, but I want you to know that I have never been truly ashamed of you until now. I thought I raised you better than this. I thought you were better than this." She sighed. "Sophia, dear, go back in your room and get your things. We're leaving."

"Is that true?" I asked as we pulled out of the driveway.

"Is what true, dear?"

"The story about Naomi and Ruth. How did I never hear about that before?" I hadn't given it much thought, but on some level I assumed there wouldn't be many stories about women loving women anywhere—especially not in the Bible. In fact, the only story I could remember ever hearing about lesbians was from my dad—the story of Sedna.

"Not everyone interprets it that way, but I do. I don't see how you could interpret it any other way," Nana answered. "But even if it wasn't true it wouldn't matter. You would still be a human being deserving of love."

I turned away so she wouldn't see the tears sliding down my cheeks. "She thinks I'm wrong or broken or... something. But I don't feel wrong."

"Baby, you're not wrong. You're not broken. She is. Her way of thinking is. There is nothing, *nothing* wrong with you. There is, however, a lot wrong with your mother. And I'm sorry I didn't do a better job of raising *her*. I'm sorry she wasn't a better mother to you. You are perfect. I love you."

"I love you, too."

"She'll come around."

"What if she doesn't?"

Nana sighed heavily. "Then you're better off without her, baby girl. You don't need her. You don't need anybody. I know you know that," she told me. "But you'll always have me." She paused. "There are some really terrible people in this world baby girl, maybe your mom is one of them, or maybe she's just confused right now. But there is so much good in you. So much value. Nothing anyone could ever say or do could rob you of that. Not even your mom."

I didn't know what to say. "Thanks, Nana."

"I wish I could fix this for you, I really do."

When we got back to her house, I holed up in the spare room. I laid on top of the made bed, staring at my phone on the pillow beside me. I wanted so badly to call Annabella and tell her what happened. We'd texted on and off every day of break so far, but I hadn't found the words to tell her that my mom kicked me out. I hadn't even told Emma yet.

It was hard enough to think it, let alone say it.

But god, I wanted to talk to her. I wanted to hear her voice. I needed to. I needed to curl up beside her and cry myself empty. I needed to feel her arms wrapped around me, her hands in my hair, her steadying heartbeat.

No, not need. I wanted it. I wanted her. What I needed was to stop thinking of people in terms of *need*. My nana was right. I knew that. I knew better than that.

I picked up my phone, let my thumb hover over the screen for a second, and put it back down on my pillow. I couldn't make myself call her, as badly as I wanted to. I was afraid that I would hear her voice and not know what to say. Or start sobbing. Or both.

But I wanted to talk to her.

I picked up my phone again. Hovered over the screen. Rolled onto my back, dropped my phone on my chest, and stared at the ceiling. Picked up the phone again. Called her. Tried to restart my heart.

She picked up after the first ring. "Sophia! How are you?"

I immediately started crying; violent sobs ripping my entire body down the middle. I felt like I was going to throw up and melt and explode and crumble all at the same time. My lungs ached. My stomach was cramping. My throat and eyes burned. There was silence on the other end of the line. I tried to stop crying and ask if she was still there but the words came out broken and mangled.

"I'm here. Let it out. Don't worry."

I cried into the phone for a solid ten minutes before I managed to calm myself enough to talk. "I'm so sorry," I said, sniffing. "I didn't mean to do that. I'm sorry."

"Don't apologize! You're okay. It's okay. Do you want to talk about it?" Annabella asked, her voice firm and level. "If you rather talk about something else, we can. Whatever you think will make you feel better, dude."

I took a deep breath, hoping that if I pulled enough air into my body there wouldn't be enough room for more water. Maybe then my body would try to hold on to what I had. I didn't want to cry anymore. I didn't think I had enough in me to cry anymore. If I lost any more liquid I'd shrivel up and die. "I told my mom. That I like girls."

"You did?" Annabella sounded surprised. "You sure don't waste any time."

"I didn't plan to… it just kind of happened."

"I take it it didn't go very well?"

"She kicked me out."

Annabella was quiet for a long time. I took the phone from my ear to make sure the call hadn't dropped. Finally, she spoke. "I'm so sorry, baby. I don't even know what to say. I'm so sorry."

"It's okay."

"What? No it isn't."

"I know."

"Where are you now? Do you need somewhere to stay? I can come get you. You can stay here. My moms won't mind," she assured me. "I can be there in like—I don't know, two and a half hours, I think?"

I shook my head, even though I knew she couldn't see me. "I'm at my nana's house. Thank you, though. I'm okay here. She's being really good. I'm okay."

"You don't sound okay."

"I'm okay."

"Sophia…"

"If I say it enough I will be. I'm okay."

"You're okay."

"I'm okay."

Silence.

"I told my moms about you, too." Annabella said finally. "And my sisters."

I sniffed. "Yeah? What did you tell them?" And what were the implications of what she told them? Her family knew she was a lesbian—so what did it mean that she told them about me specifically?

"I told them about how beautiful you are. How good I feel when I'm around you. How funny you are…" she hesitated. "How when I touch you I can feel every cell in my body light up."

My heart jumped up into my throat.

"I miss you."

I swallowed my heart. "I miss you, too." I picked up the old quilt and started pulling at the unraveling strings. All the words I wanted to say to her turned to sand in my mouth. The grains slid down my throat and out of the corners of my mouth, but formed nothing of substance. I was over the moon that she felt that way, too, but somehow still too embarrassed to tell her. There was a crawling fluttering jittery tickling feeling in the pit of my stomach. Like the spiders but lighter. Almost pleasant.

I had butterflies for the first time in years.

I bit my lip to keep a smile from forming. A tiny laugh escaped despite my efforts.

"What are you thinking about?"

I pulled another string. "Nothing, I don't know."

"C'mon, Soph, tell me," she pleaded. "I wanna know."

I couldn't hold in my smile anymore. "I was just thinking about how I have butterflies right now thinking about you."

"You do?"

"Yeah," I said, my face hot.

She giggled. "You are so fucking cute, holy shit."

"Oh my god, stop. You are the cutest."

"I want to kiss you."

My heart skipped a beat. "I want to kiss you, too."

"Yeah?"

"Yeah, I do."

"What a shame that you're so far from me, then," Annabella said. "I want to hold you and play with your hair and kiss your face."

The butterflies in my stomach exploded. "I want that, too. So much."

"What are you doing tomorrow? Maybe I could come visit you."

"You would drive all the way here just to kiss me?"

Annabella laughed. "I'm pretty sure that I would drive all the way across the country to kiss you, Sophia," she told me. "I like you so much."

"I like you too." An entire garden bloomed inside of me when I said it. Lilies and daisies and orchids and roses and tulips. With butterflies and honeybees to boot. I could feel their petals and leaves and wings tickling my insides.

"So tomorrow?"

I smiled. "I'd like that a lot."

thirteen
annabella morgan avery
March 27

Driving down to Sophia's was weirdly therapeutic. It was, for the most part, a straight shot down 495 all the way to the very beginning of Cape Cod. I'd been to the Cape once before, when I was about nine. I remembered that drive as tedious and exhausting. This time, it was exhilarating and calming at the same time.

I couldn't wait to see her. I couldn't wait to kiss her.

My fingers migrated up towards my face, brushing over my lips. Something in my chest fluttered when I thought about kissing her. My head felt like it was floating away. If I wasn't careful, I'd veer off the road.

I didn't really have a plan of action, per say. I didn't know what I was going to do. I didn't know what was going to come out of my trip to her nana's house. I didn't know what my willingness to drive two and a half hours to see her even meant. All I knew was that I wanted to see her. I wanted to spend fifty bucks in gas money to drive down to this town I'd never been to before to see this girl I met less than a month ago. I wanted to. I wanted to be around her.

I wanted *her*.

Which was both amazing and terrifying.

I wondered what she was thinking about right then. If she was glancing at the clock every thirty-seven seconds like I was. Counting down the minutes. If her stomach was preforming the same acrobatic feats that mine was.

I needed to take my mind off it somehow. I wasn't sure that that was even possible, but driving myself insane with nerves wasn't going to help anything. I wasn't used to someone making me feel like this. Making me feel so alive and just... like every molecule in my body was vibrating with energy. I felt like I was radiating light. There was so much in me and all I wanted was to give it to her.

Her nana's house was bigger than I imagined it would be. The exterior walls were cranberry red, but the front door was a soft blue. It was an unusual paring, but it looked nice somehow. Messy, overgrown evergreen bushes lined the stone pathway to the front door. Something about them added charm.

I rang the doorbell and stepped back. I could feel my heartbeat everywhere from the soles of my feet to the top of my head. My fingers wrapped around a small branch from the bush behind me and bent it back, snapping off a small piece. I found myself ripping off the needles while I waited for someone to answer the door.

I lived and died on that front step before Sophia finally opened the door. I dropped the naked twig on the ground in surprise.

"Annabella!" It was amazing to hear her voice. Somehow, she managed to melt away all of the pent up anxiety inside of me. She wrapped her arms around me and my heartbeat settled. "How was the drive?" she asked, pulling away. Her hand was still on my arm and I was hyperaware of it.

"It was good. How are you?"

"I'm good, what about you?"

"Great." I smiled. "Is your nana here?"

She shook her head. "No, she just left actually. She'll be back in an hour or two," she said, leading me inside. "Why?"

"Just curious. I wanted to meet her." I shrugged, looking around the house. It was cluttered and disorganized in the most charming way. How long did you have to live to acquire so much *stuff*? There were several lifetimes' worth of belongings crammed into this house, and yet it somehow managed to look welcoming and homey and not overwhelming. I couldn't imagine ever owning that many things, let alone all at the same time.

Sophia led me into the kitchen, which was marginally less cluttered. "Do you want anything to eat or drink?" she asked, opening the cabinet and getting herself a glass.

"Water would be great, thanks." She took down another glass. I wandered over to the fridge and started looking at the pictures. About half of them were clearly Sophia at different ages. The other half was divided among three other very similar-looking white girls and a baby boy. I wondered if they were her cousins. "Who are they?"

Sophia handed me a glass. "My cousins. Noah, Charlie, Scout, Jacob." She pointed to each in turn.

"All boys' names?"

She shrugged. "My uncle is a narcissist. He wanted a boy," she gestured to the baby boy again. "Once he finally got him, he even named him after himself." She made a face, something torn between amusement and disgust. "I don't really see them much. They live in Connecticut." She explained. "So. What do you feel like doing? We can't really go out anywhere until my nana gets back with the car, because you don't know where anything is here and it's easier if I drive... I don't know. I'm a really terrible hostess, sorry." Sophia laughed nervously.

"Anything. Nothing. I'm not really concerned with what we do. I'm just happy to see you," I told her earnestly.

Sophia smiled, then immediately covered her face with her fingers, like she was embarrassed of it. I reached up and pulled her hand away, intertwining my fingers with hers. She looked away, still smiling.

"Hey, Sophia."

She looked at me, biting her lip. "What?"

"Kiss me."

She laughed and pecked me on the cheek. I felt a flower bloom there where her lips touched me.

I was overcome with the desire to push her against the fridge and kiss her, but I resisted. I wanted her so badly. I wanted everything else to disappear and for things to be easier. I wanted all the weights holding me down to disappear and for me to stop being such an *idiot* and stop overthinking this.

I wanted her.

"You missed," I told her.

Still laughing, she kissed me again, on the lips this time. The sound was so sweet and so pure that I couldn't help but laugh, too. We dissolved into a fit of giggles and she wrapped her arms around me. I felt like I was full of bubbles. If she let go of me, I would float up to the ceiling and burst.

As it was, my heart felt like it might burst anyway. I squeezed her. I couldn't get close enough.

We ended up curled up on the oversized, overstuffed couch in her nana's living room. A thick quilt was draped over us to stave off the cold, but Sophia was more or less a space heater in her own right. The lights were off and the shades were drawn and it was easy to forget that there were people besides us that existed outside.

We'd decided on some Swedish movie my Moms told me was good, but I couldn't focus on it. I was melting into her, my head resting on her chest and her arm draped over me. She was absently playing with my fingers, seemingly unaware of the tiny fireworks she was setting off under my skin. My hand that she wasn't playing with was tracing circles on a slice of skin her sweater rode up over.

I hoped that she was having a similar reaction to my touch.

The blonde femme in the movie was kissing the neck of the brunette femme. Sophia squeezed my hand and I looked up at her, once again amazed at how beautiful she was. Blinded by it. She pecked me on the lips. I couldn't suppress the giggle building in my throat as I sat up a little straighter to kiss her. My hand slid up her side, brushing the bare skin under her sweater. I was astounded by how soft she was. How smooth her skin was.

She pulled me closer to her. I felt like I was starving. Sophia kissed me harder, her hand finding its way into my hair. I felt like my heart was going to stop beating. My fingers brushed the edge of her bra, but I didn't dare let myself go any further. I could feel her smiling.

The lights turned on and the room instantly went cold. I ducked down and pulled the blankets over my face, mortified. "Oh—I hope I'm not interrupting anything," a woman said. "No need to hide, sweetheart." She laughed. "Sophia, tell your friend to come out."

Sophia's hand sought out mine under the blankets. When she found it, she squeezed. "Annabella." I peeked out from under the covers, my face hot. "This is my Nana, Rosemarie. Nana, this is Annabella."

"You can call me Anna," I said, glancing at Sophia.

"Nice to meet you, Anna. I hope you like vegetarian lasagna." She held up her grocery bags. She looked nothing like I imagined. Tall and wiry

with peach skin and stark white hair. She didn't
even come close to resembling the cluttered,
disorganized woman I was expecting based on her
home. She dressed simply, not eclectically, and her
hair was cut short and well kept. She looked warm,
though. Like Sophia.

"I do, thank you. I hope you didn't go to any
trouble over me."

Rosemarie shook her head. "Nonsense. It's
no trouble at all. I'm happy to have you here.
Sophia told me a lot about you." She smiled. I
squeezed Sophia's hand under the covers. "Well,
I'll leave you two alone now and go start dinner.
Let me know if you need anything." And with that,
she disappeared into the kitchen.

"She seems sweet," I said.

"She is." Sophia kissed the top of my head.

Her nana stuck her head around the corner.
"Annabella, dear, are you spending the night?" I
glanced at Sophia, who shrugged. "You're more
than welcome to, just let me know. I'll make up the
spare bed for you." She disappeared again.

"Do you want me to stay?"

Sophia laughed. "What do you think?"

We decided to go out while her nana made
dinner. Sophia didn't say where she was taking me,
but she seemed excited about it. When we got in the
car, she pulled a cd out of the glove compartment
and put it in.

"I made this cd for you," she said. "Is that
weird or lame or…? If it is just pretend I didn't."

She laughed nervously as the first track started to play.

I smiled hard. "No, oh my god, that's so sweet. I make people cds all the time. I don't think anyone has ever made one for me," I told her. "Thank you so much."

"Don't thank me until after you hear it. I don't even know what kind of music you like."

"I like this song."

"Yeah?"

"Yeah, I do." We backed out of the driveway. "Where are we going?"

"One of my favorite places. I've never brought anyone there before. That's all I'm gonna say."

The drive took a little over half an hour, and Sophia and I spent most of it in a comfortable silence. I spent most of it wishing I could hold her hand.

We pulled off the road somewhere empty looking and turned into a gravel parking lot. There were no buildings around, no people, no anything. Just some sort of (clearly man-made) river and an abundance of trees. Sophia reached into the back of the car and pulled a sweatshirt out from behind the seat.

"Here." She handed it to me. "The sun's gonna set soon. It's gonna get cold." She explained. "Your sweatshirt isn't very thick."

I unzipped my hoodie and slid out of it, replacing it with hers. When I looked down to find my seatbelt and unbuckle, I took a deep breath and realized that it smelled exactly like her.

She was right about the cold. As soon as I got out of the car I could feel the bitter air biting my cheeks and nose. Luckily, though, it wasn't windy. Even the slightest breeze would've sent the frozen air straight through my skin like a knife. It would have shattered my bones.

We headed towards the river then, crossing a dirty old bridge that, despite the missing boards, felt impossibly sturdy. The water below us rushed over a small ledge, splashing heavily on the rocks below. I felt Sophia's hand slide into mine and suddenly, I wasn't cold anymore. The heat reawakened the butterflies in my stomach.

God, I had it bad.

The trees came right up to the bridge on the other side. They were tall and sparse, with thin, gray trunks stretching up to the sky. Their branches started several feet above my head, forming a canopy. The shrubs below were just starting to green up after a long, cold winter. Bringing life back to the otherwise grayed forest.

Sophia rubbed her thumb against mine. The air between us was alive with static and buzzing, red hot atoms. I could feel every millimeter of space between our arms. Every increase in distance from our hands up. The deep V that sliced between us. I nudged her with my shoulder, momentarily closing it, but that only led me to feel it even more strongly when we parted again.

"So where exactly are you taking me? Into the woods to kill me?" I joked.

Sophia laughed. "How did you know?"

"Intuition." I smirked. She squeezed my hand again. "But seriously, where are you taking me? It doesn't seem like there's much of anything out here."

"You'll see, just be patient." She squeezed my hand again.

The woods around us grew thicker and thicker as we progressed, until we were walking a defined trail through the trees that we couldn't really stray from. The trail narrowed as we went on, forcing us closer together and closer together. Closing the V of space that came between our arms.

Not that I minded.

Suddenly, the trees parted and opened up to a large clearing. Thick, soft looking grass sprung up in the space between the trees, looking out of place among the undergrowth. Towards one edge of the clearing, there was an old, worn out looking bench.

"It's not much," Sophia said. "Sorry if I overhyped it. But this is kind of just. My place. I come here whenever I'm stressed or worried or just... need to be alone." She glanced down at me. "Like I said, I've never brought anyone here before. I've never even felt the need to. But... I don't know. I wanted to bring you. Sorry if it's lame."

"It's not lame at all," I said, turning to face her and takin her other hand in mine. "Thank you for sharing this with me. It means a lot." I wrapped my arms around her waist and pulled her to me, my head pressed up against her chest. I could hear her heartbeat.

She hugged me back, her warmth seeping into my bones. Something in me felt... settled.

My body felt quiet. My head and heart felt safe.

fourteen

sophia jane kalvak
March 27

We stayed in the clearing until well after the sun had set, holding each other on the bench and talking about the most mundane of things. Somehow, though, our conversations felt so meaningful to me. When my nana texted me to tell me that dinner was ready, I almost wanted to pretend I didn't see it. I didn't want to break the spell. Even though I knew she wasn't leaving yet, even though I knew we would be together tomorrow and then back at school in a few days, something about leaving the clearing there felt like an end.

I knew we would have to talk about Us, capital u, sooner or later. But I didn't want that just yet. I wasn't ready for that. I was content to just let things be as they were for now. For now, things felt perfect.

We drove home in the same comfortable, safe silence that we departed in. The cd I made her played softly in the background, and I held her hand over the center consol. It felt weird at first, holding someone's hand while driving, but then I thought about how it was *Annabella's* hand, and I had never been more comfortable driving one-handed.

The rest of the night was low-key. We ate dinner with my nana, endured her embarrassing questions, and spent most of the night curled up together on the couch pretending to watch movies. As hard as I tried to focus on the events taking place onscreen, all I could pay attention to was the way her body felt up against mine. The little currents of electricity passing between us.

When it was time to go to bed, I kissed her on the cheek and led her to the guest room like my nana told us. It was agony letting go of her. Every single cell in my body lurched forward towards her, but I had to pull back.

I crawled into my own bed afterwards, feeling small and cold. I pulled the blanket up to my chin and wrapped it tightly around my body. It didn't seem to do anything to quell the cold.

I laid on my back, staring up at the ceiling, for what felt like several hours. But when I turned to look at the clock, it had only been about ten minutes. I thought about Annabella lying alone in the other room and my heart skipped a beat.

My chest ached.

The door creaked open. "Sophia?"

My heart stopped.

"I know I'm supposed to be in the other room…"

"Come here."

I didn't look as she crossed the room, her footsteps soft on the carpet. I slid over in the bed, propping myself up on my side. Annabella crawled into bed with me, pulling the blanket over herself. She pressed herself up against me, her head resting on my arm. I draped my other arm over her, pulling her close to me. Our legs intertwined and our bodies seemed to melt into one. It was hard to tell where I ended and she began.

We didn't talk, really. We just held each other. Every couple minutes, she would stretch her neck and kiss me on the nose or the cheek or the lips, or squeeze me tighter, or brush hair from my face. Tiny displays of affection. Tiny pieces of her attention. Just enough to light my insides on fire and make me wonder how I could have survived this long thinking I was straight.

How did I manage to deny myself this? No boy's touch had ever managed to make me feel this way. She was so soft, so precious. I wanted to hold her for the rest of my life. I wanted to take care of her. To cherish her. To worship her. She was a goddess. Her beauty was astounding. Her touch was intoxicating.

It wasn't until that moment that I realized how truly, how completely, how desperately I wanted to be with her. How I wanted to be hers in every conceivable way. How I was so, so glad to be friends with her, but so desperate for more at the same time.

I wanted to kiss her for the rest of my life. I knew it was foolish and childish and that life just didn't work that way, but I did. I was never the one for sweeping, idealistic romance, but something about Annabella made me think that it could be real. That I could have that kind of fairytale happiness.

It was foolish. I was foolish. But I was so, so happy.

Despite my desperate attempts to not be tired, I yawned. I felt like my body had betrayed me. Ignored my every wish and admitted that I couldn't stay awake with her forever.

"Sleepy?" she asked. Her voice was slow and heavy, like she was on the brink of falling asleep herself.

"Kind of," I admitted.

"Go to bed, silly."

"I don't want to," I said, stifling another yawn. I wasn't ready to go to sleep. I wasn't sure I would ever really be ready.

She raised an eyebrow. "Why not?"

"Because I want to be with you still," I told her quietly. My face felt hot. Saying the words out loud was more embarrassing than just feeling them. I wanted to spend every waking second with her. And I wanted most of my seconds to be waking seconds. I wanted all the time with her that I could get.

She laughed, sitting up slightly and kissing my forehead. "Dream about me, then." She nestled her head back between my arm and my chest, draping an arm over my stomach. "I'll dream about you, too."

Something inside me fluttered violently as I turned to press my lips against her hairline. "Okay."

"Sweet dreams," she said, sounding like she was already halfway gone. I kissed her nose and then her lips. She smiled and scooted closer to me. I had the feeling that even if she was on top of me, Annabella would never truly be close enough. Every inch of me was craving every inch of her. I couldn't get enough. Did she feel the same?

"Sweet dreams," I echoed, closing my heavy eyelids. I took a deep breath, drunk off the scent of her shampoo. I thought that if I died right then and there, I would have died the happiest woman on earth.

I woke up before she did the next morning, my hair sticking to my face and my arm dead asleep under her. The clock on the nightstand beside us told me that it was nearly ten am. Annabella shifted beside me, a low humming sound slipping out of her lips. I glanced down to see if she was waking up. Her eyes were still shut, but she was smiling.

My nana would be awake soon, if she wasn't already. I didn't want her to know that Annabella had spent the night in my bed.

I brushed Annabella's tangled curls away from her face and pressed my lips to her forehead. "Annabella."

"Mmm?" She didn't open her eyes, but she did close the small space between our chests.

"Good morning," I said, running my hand through her hair, brushing the rest of it away from her face. "I don't want to wake you, but I don't want my nana to know you slept in here."

Annabella opened her eyes. "Oh, right. I forgot about that." She sat up, stretching. "Sorry."

"No, don't be sorry. I'm glad you came," I told her as she pulled her hair up in a messy bun on the top of her head. "It was nice."

"It was."

"Did you sleep well?" I asked, sitting up and shaking my dead arm a little. The skin on my right side was sticky with half-dried sweat.

Annabella nodded. "I did. Better than I have in a while, actually," she told me. "You make me feel safe. I don't have to worry about anything when I'm with you." She laughed a little. I could listen to her laugh for the rest of my life and never get tired of it. "I know it sounds silly."

"No, it doesn't. I know what you mean. You make me feel safe, too. And brave. Like nothing can hurt me," I said. I was fully expecting my stomach to flip and my cheeks to burn but nothing happened. I wasn't embarrassed. "I'm so glad I met you, Annabella."

"I'm glad I met you, too, Sophia."

My stomach fluttered and she slid her hand into mine, rubbing her thumb on the back of my hand.

"Sophia." My nana poked her head into the room, startling me. "Oh! I didn't realize you were both up," she said, glancing at Annabella before returning her gaze to me. "Did you girls want breakfast?"

I looked over at Annabella, who nodded. "Yeah, sure. What are you making?"

"How about we go out? My treat."

"Oh, no, I can pay for myself. Thank you though."

"Nonsense." My nana shook her head. "Get dressed, we'll leave as soon as you're ready." She smiled, disappearing from the room and closing the door behind her.

"So what are you majoring in dear?" Nana asked once we were in the car. "And what do you want to do once you graduate?"

Annabella laughed. "The worst question. I'm double majoring in psychology and women's studies. I have no idea really what I want to do once I graduate, though. Something in the field of counseling but I haven't decided. I've got to get my masters and all that first, though, so I guess I have time to figure it out."

"Oh really? I actually have my BA in psychology." Nana said. "I did social work for about a decade and a half."

"Oh really? That's awesome. I was thinking about going into social work a while back. Before I added my women's studies major. Now I think I wanna do something more along the lines of advocacy for survivors of domestic abuse. But I'm not sure."

"Interesting. Do you have plans to go to law school? That would probably help you in that respect."

"I've been thinking about that lately, actually. But like I said, I'm not sure yet. I guess I should work on figuring things out more definitively soon, though." She laughed. "It's a bit daunting."

Nana laughed. "That it is. But you can always change your career path if you find you aren't in love with it. Lord knows I did several times. Things aren't ever set in stone," she told her.

The restaurant was fairly empty, as one would expect on a Friday morning. A large, grizzled looking man sat at the counter nursing a large mug of coffee and staring straight ahead. An elderly couple sat in the far corner, sharing a plate of pancakes. An exhausted looking mother pushed her fussy infant's stroller back and forth as she circled things with a red marker in the newspaper.

We were seated in a booth near the elderly couple, Nana on one side and Annabella and I on the other. The waitress handed us our menus and took our drink orders. She was beautiful, but I didn't think I'd ever seen anyone look so tired in my entire life. Her thick, coarse black hair was pulled tight into a bun on the back of her head and she wore bags under her almost black eyes. I wondered when her last day off was. She looked exhausted. I watched her disappear into the kitchen, then turned my attention back to Annabella.

She held my hand under the table. Something about it felt so secret and important, even though my nana knew who she was to me. There was this hidden sense of intimacy from this display of affection that no one else could see or feel. Even something so minute, so inconsequential, as holding hands. I could feel the hairs on my arms stand up.

Nana started rambling on about some article she read somewhere, as she often did. I listened with one ear; a miniscule portion of my attention. The rest was focused on the feeling of her hand in mine, her knee touching mine, the atoms buzzing between us. I felt like I was charged with a thousand volts of electricity. If I touched the metal screw on the side of the booth with my free hand, I'd shock us all.

The waitress, whose nametag said Tzipporah, brought us our drinks and set them down on the table in front of us. After she took our orders I made sure to give her the most earnest 'thank you' and smile that I could muster. She smiled back warmly.

"So will you be staying another night or are you going to head home today?" Nana asked. "Either is fine with me, of course."

Annabella hesitated, glancing at me. "I think I should probably head home this afternoon." She squeezed my hand under the table. "My sister's birthday is today and I promised I'd take her out tonight," she explained. "Though if you want to come back with me, I wouldn't say no." She laughed. "Can't promise I'd bring you back, though."

I laughed.

"I think you should go with her, Sophia," Nana said. "It's no good for you to stay cooped up with me for the rest of your break. That is, if you were serious and your mother and father would be okay with it," she added, looking at Annabella.

"Of course I was serious. And my moms wouldn't mind." Annabella looked at me. "Do you want to come with me? Moms are dying to meet you anyway. Might as well bite the bullet and get it over with," she joked. "It's okay if you don't wanna. You can say no."

"I'd love to," I said. "I'd love to meet your family. Are you sure your moms wouldn't mind having me? I don't want to intrude," I told her, suddenly feeling anxious about it. What if her moms didn't like me? What if Annabella got sick of me after spending so much time with me?

"I want you to come, Soph. You're not intruding." All the voices in my head quieted instantly.

"Okay. I'll come with you." I rubbed my thumb on hers, squeezing.

Annabella grinned. "Good."

Tzipporah brought us our food then. "Enjoy, you guys. Let me know if you need anything." We all thanked her and she disappeared into the kitchen again.

We ate in silence for the most part, too hungry to maintain small talk. When we were finished eating my nana paid and I left a $20 on the table for Tzipporah. I couldn't explain why I felt the need to tip her that much, but I felt good about it. I hoped it brightened her day, at least.

I wanted someone else to feel as good as I was feeling.

Annabella and I decided to leave almost immediately after getting back to my nana's house. I packed up my things, kissed Nana on the cheek and thanked her for everything she did for me, and we were off less than an hour later.

She held my hand almost the entire way there.

fifteen
annabella morgan avery
March 28

I called Ma once we were almost to my house to tell her that Sophia was coming over. I didn't want them to have too much time to prepare. I didn't want them to go overboard like they always seemed to when they were excited. It was cute and endearing and all, but I was 98% sure that it would unnerve Sophia. Who seemed anxious enough to begin with.

We pulled into the driveway and I turned the car off but didn't move right away. "I'd just like to formally apologize right now for whatever embarrassing thing my moms do today. We'll take Liliana out for dinner in like, two or three hours. We won't be there too long. Just. Bear with me," I said, laughing nervously. It hadn't occurred to me that I would be the anxious one here.

"Don't worry about it, Annabella," Sophia said, smiling. "I'm sure they're great. I'm sure I'll love them."

"I'm sure they'll love you, too." I hesitated. "Is this weird?"

"Is what weird?"

"I don't know." I shook my head. "Is it weird to bring you home to meet my parents? I mean. We're not... dating or anything. Is it weird?" I asked, feeling something black start to fester in my chest.

Sophia shrugged. "I don't think it's weird. Friends meet each other's parents, right?" Her voice was quiet, though. I bit down on the inside of my cheek. "It's fine, you're overthinking it."

"I'm overthinking everything," I admitted. "I'm sorry. I know I'm making this more complicated than it needs to be."

"Making what more complicated?"

"Everything."

Sophia leaned over the center console and kissed me on the cheek. "You're fine, Annabella. Stop worrying. Everything is fine."

"You sure?"

"I'm positive," Sophia said, unbuckling her seatbelt. "Now let's go inside. I want to meet your moms."

The festering in my chest settled down a bit, but didn't go away completely. Sophia got out of the car and shut the door behind her. I got out, too, even though no part of me felt ready. I didn't want to keep her waiting. I was doing enough of that.

When we got inside, Ma was making herself a sandwich in the kitchen. Mom was reading at the table, her legs propped up on the chair across from her. I tried to make as little noise as possible coming in, but as soon as the door creaked open, both their heads shot up. I felt something in me drop.

Why was I so anxious?

"Hey, Anna," Ma said. "And you must be Sophia." She wiped her hands on her jeans and walked towards us, arms outstretched. I glanced nervously at Sophia as Ma embraced her. Sophia smiled and hugged her back. "We're so happy to have you! How was the drive up, girls?"

"It was good, Ma. No traffic or anything," I said. Mom put her book and got up from the table. She leaned over the counter, propped up on her elbows.

"Nice to finally meet you, Sophia. We've heard so much about you," Mom said. "All good things, of course."

I rolled my eyes. "Sophia, this is Calliope." I gestured to Mom, "And this is Eleanor," I said, pointing to Ma. "My moms." They both grinned.

"It's really nice to meet you guys, too. Thank you so much for having me," Sophia said.

Ma walked around the counter to stand next to Mom, leaning forward on her elbows, too, so their arms were touching. "So what's the plan for you guys today? Doing anything for Liliana's birthday?" she asked.

"Yeah, we're gonna take her out to dinner later. As for right now…" I glanced at Sophia. "I don't really know. I'm pretty tired from driving. We'll probably just hang out in my room or something."

Mom frowned. "Well don't be strangers, girls. Your mother and I are staying in tonight and we want to spend some time with you before you go back to school. Maybe after you get back from dinner we can play a board game or watch a movie or something." Ma laughed. "What? I like board games. You're just mad that you never win." Mom laughed, nudging Ma lightly.

"Oh, I let you win," Ma joked.

"You do *not*."

Ma laughed again. "Sure I do. All the time. You're a sore loser and a cute winner." Mom kissed her on the cheek. I made a gagging noise. "What, too gay?" Ma winked at me.

"We're gonna go in my room now bye," I said quickly, grabbing Sophia by the arm and leading her down the hall. I shut the bedroom door behind us.

"They're cute," Sophia said as I threw myself down on my bed. She sat beside me, on the edge. "I like them."

"They're... a lot," I said. "But they're good."

"Well, I think they're cute. I mean they're your moms so I guess it makes sense that you wouldn't. But it's... nice. They love each other a lot, I can tell. That's nice. Reassuring. I don't know."

"What do you mean?" I sat up.

Sophia shrugged. "I don't know. I didn't exactly grow up with a lot of gay people around me. I grew up being told that gay people are… sick. Degenerate. That they didn't get happy endings. But your moms look really happy together. It's nice to see. I don't know." She shook her head. "I don't want to believe my mom because being around you and how I feel about you feels… right. I don't feel bad. I don't feel broken. But it's something I have to unlearn still, I guess." She brushed her fingers against my arm absently.

"That makes sense," I said, but I knew I would never really understand where she was coming from. I was so lucky. So, so lucky. I touched her hair, twisting the tendrils between my fingers. "We're not broken."

"I know."

"Good," I said, pecking her on the cheek.

"You missed."

I pecked her on the lips.

"Better." She laughed. I winked at her. She laughed again. Somewhere in my ribs, calla lilies began to blossom.

We napped together, curled up into each other under a pile of blankets, until almost 5:30. When I woke up, Sophia was wrapped around me, head heavy on my chest. I kissed the top of her head. "Hey, Sophia. Wake up, we gotta get ready to take Liliana out." I kissed her again. "You've gotta be awake to deal with her."

Sophia blinked her eyes open slowly, looking up at me through her lashes. "What time is it?" she asked.

"About half past five. We should get going soon." Sophia nuzzled her head into my chest. "Don't do that," I laughed. "It's her birthday. C'mon." I kissed her forehead. "Stop being so cute, we have to get out of this bed."

Sophia giggled. "Sorry, can't stop being cute. But I guess we can get up." She squeezed me tight before untangling herself from me and rolling out of bed. I watched her straighten her clothes and fix her hair, practically mesmerized, before I got up myself. She brushed my hair out of my face carefully, then fixed my part for me. I tried not to smile too much.

"Thanks for fixing my hair."

"Thanks for calling me cute."

"Thanks for being cute."

Sophia smiled, then covered her face with her hands. I pulled them away from her face and stood on my tip toes to kiss her nose. "Come on cutie, we gotta go. Liliana's probably starving."

We picked Liliana up from her best friend, Lila's house. She got in the backseat of Ma's car, hanging over my seat and resting her head on the back of it. "Is this Sophia?" She jerked her thumb in her direction. I nodded. Liliana stuck her hand out to Sophia. "Nice to meet you. This idiot doesn't shut up about you." She laughed. "It's good to put a face to it."

"*Lil*," I groaned.

Sophia laughed. "It's nice to meet you too, Liliana. You're not nearly as awful as Annabella said you were."

"Aw, you oversold me *again,* Anna? I'm never gonna make an impression this way. You have to tone it down." Liliana rolled her eyes.

"Sorry, kid. I'll try harder next time," I laughed. "Where do you wanna go for dinner?"

Liliana shrugged, sitting back in her seat. "Doesn't matter as long as you're paying, sis." She smirked. "I'm kind of leaning towards Japanese or Thai, though. But I could go for anything," she said. "I'm starving."

"Ooh, Thai sounds good," Sophia said.

"Thai it is," I agreed, backing out of the driveway and heading towards town.

As was to be expected, the restaurant was packed when we got there. We had to wait about twenty minutes for a table, much to Liliana's annoyance. She whined in my ear almost the entire time, if not because she was actually irritated then because she just felt like irritating *me.*

Liliana and I were regulars at House of Thai. The waitress recognized us immediately and took down our usual orders—pad Thai with tofu. "And what can I get you, dear?" she asked Sophia.

"Water to drink. And pad Thai is good, thanks."

"Alright! I'll be right back with your drinks." She grinned at us before heading off.

"So, how has your birthday been so far?" Sophia asked. "How old are you?"

"I'm sixteen. And it's been alright. Nothing special. Went to school. Went to Lila's. Now I'm here." She shrugged. "Meeting the girl my sister is gaga over is probably the most exciting thing that's happened to me today. So congrats on that one," she said dryly.

Sophia frowned. "Sorry you're not having a great day."

Lil laughed. "No dude, it's fine. This is a good day. Just not extraordinarily good, you know?" She shrugged. "No big deal."

"Jeez, Lil, tone it down dude. You're too ecstatic. It's too much. Settle down." I rolled my eyes. "What's with the angst, baby?" I asked as the waitress brought our drinks.

"I'm not angsty," Lil said. "Just being honest. It was a boring day."

"Well what can we do to make it better, then?"

Liliana shrugged. "No idea. I'm not mad about it or anything. Don't worry, dude."

"Alright, then…" I shook my head. "Anyway, Moms want to hang with all of us tonight. Probably Char, too," I told her. "So that should be… fun."

"Excellent. We haven't had a painfully embarrassing family night in ages." Liliana looked at Sophia. "And with a guest, too! You're in for a treat." She laughed.

Sophia shrugged. "It can't be that bad. Your moms seem really nice. I don't mind spending time with them." She frowned, looking at her hands. *Fuck, her mom just kicked her out.* I felt like hitting myself on the head. *It probably stings at least a little to see us all... happy and shit. And taking it for granted.* I took her hand under the table and squeezed. She looked up from her hands and smiled. Lil rolled her eyes and I kicked her shin.

I played with my straw wrapper while Liliana and Sophia played twenty questions, listening to Sophia's answers while halfheartedly predicting my baby sister's. I was right about nine times out of ten with her. And every time Sophia gave an answer something in me went *of course.*

The waitress brought our food and their question game continued.

"Favorite movie?" Liliana asked.

Sophia paused the longest at that one. "I'm bad at committing to favorite anythings. I guess the first Narnia movie. Me and dad used to watch it together all the time. Then when he died me and mom always watched it." Her voice got quieter and quieter as her explanation progressed. Liliana gave me a confused look but I just shook my head. "What's yours?" she asked, shaking her head too as if to shake the thoughts from her mind.

"Hmm. I'm not a big movie person. I like anything with Will Smith, though. Not because he's an amazing actor or anything. He's just nice to look at." She laughed.

I made a face.

"Sorry, too hetero?" Liliana raised an eyebrow.

"Entirely too hetero. It's fine if you're straight, Lil, just don't shove it in my face, okay? There are like... *kids* here." I laughed.

Liliana laughed, too. Sophia raised her eyebrow at me and I just laughed harder. That was exactly the face Cora made when we joked about it around her. She didn't get the need to joke about it. She thought it was silly.

"You gotta joke about it sometime. It makes it easier."

When we got home, Moms already had Monopoly set up on the kitchen table, along with five glasses and a bottle of red wine. There was a birthday cake on the counter, along with two wrapped gifts—one from them, and one from Char and me. Moms and Char were all sitting at the counter behind the cake.

"Happy birthday!" Moms yelled in unison. Cora chimed in a little late. Ma lit the candles on the cake and Mom started the singing. Liliana rolled her eyes through the entire spectacle. When she blew out the candles, Mom snapped a picture, much to my little sister's chagrin.

We ate cake together, but Liliana insisted on opening her presents on her own later. For a girl with blue hair, she wasn't too big on the public spectacle thing. She cited something about wanting to keep her reactions to herself or some other melodramatic sixteen year old excuse.

When we finished eating, Moms shepherded us to the dining room table to play Monopoly.

"Sophia can pick first because she's the guest," Mom said.

"Oh, I don't really—"

"Just pick," Liliana said, rolling her eyes yet again. She was pouting because Mom wouldn't let her have a glass of wine. But I saw Ma sneak her a sip when Mom's back was turned.

Sophia grabbed the first piece her fingers came in contact with, the thimble. We went clockwise then, everyone picking a stupid metal object to represent them on the game board. I drained my glass a little too quickly and had Char refill it for me.

Monopoly lasted entirely too long for my taste and for my attention span. Another glass and a half of wine later and I had about had it with it. "Sophia, let's consolidate."

"What?"

"Here," I handed over all my properties and money. "We're a team now."

"You can't do that!" Liliana protested.

"Sure I can. We're married in Monopoly now." I kissed her on the cheek for emphasis. "What's mine is hers."

Mom laughed. "Fair enough, but no way am I consolidating with you, Eleanor. I love you dearly but I also want to kick your ass."

"I don't know about kicking, but you can certainly kiss my ass, Calliope." Ma made kissing noises at Mom, who was laughing and pushing her back.

Sophia laughed, laying her head on my shoulder. Maybe it was the wine or maybe it was her laugh or maybe it was a combination of the two, but I found myself once again astounded and in awe of how beautiful she was. How kind she was. How warm she was. How safe she was.

My entire body was buzzing with affection for this girl. This beautiful amazing hilarious sweet safe perfect girl. This beautiful amazing hilarious sweet safe perfect girl who felt the same way about me. This beautiful amazing hilarious sweet safe perfect girl who felt the same way about me and who was still hanging around me even though I was an idiot who couldn't get out of her own head for long enough to realize what she had right in front of her. I was buzzing and I wanted her so badly that I could feel it in every nanometer of my body and all I could think was *why not*? Why not be hers? What was I waiting for?

What was I *doing*?

sixteen
sophia jane kalvak
March 28

My hands were shaking as I sat on the bathroom floor, phone in hand. It seemed so stupid. So idiotic. So unfathomably ill-advised. My heart was already so broken and bruised, I wasn't sure it could take another run-in with my mother. But it was because my heart was so broken and bruised that I felt compelled to sit on the cold bathroom floor at 11:30 pm and call her.

I was a little drunk, but I didn't think she would notice. Truthfully, I didn't even think she would pick up.

I held the phone to my ear, my heartbeat skyrocketing. The ringing sounded so distant. Like I was holding the phone across the room instead of against my ear. I felt so removed and to invested at the same time. The tear occurred somewhere down my middle. I looked down at my stomach to be sure that my organs weren't spilling out onto the blue tiled floor.

There was a click. The line went dead. No voice. No voicemail. No nothing.

I pulled the phone away from my face and looked at the screen. Maybe the call dropped. Maybe she hung up by accident. Maybe. Maybe. Maybe.

I called her again.

Click. Emptiness.

Again.

Click. Nothing.

Tears in my eyes, I tried one last time. It went straight to voicemail.

At the tone, feel free to record your message. When you are finished recording, hang up or press one for more options. Beep.

"Mom?" I swallowed my tears. "It's Sophia." I felt so stupid. I didn't even know why I was leaving her a message. She wouldn't listen to it. She wouldn't care. "I don't know why I'm calling you. I wanted you to call me. I wanted you to tell me you were sorry and you loved me. I wanted you to tell me that you loved me still. But you don't, do you?" Something in my throat snagged. "You're supposed to love me unconditionally. Why can't you do that?"

The line beeped to tell me that I'd used up all my time, but I couldn't stop.

"Why can't you just love me, mom? I'm not going to apologize. I didn't do anything wrong. I'm not broken, you are. You are. I'm not hurting anyone. You are. You're supposed… you're supposed to love people. That's what god wants, right?" My voice cracked. "I'm not broken, you are." The phone slid out of my hands and I buried my face in them, sobbing.

Someone knocked on the door but I pretended I didn't hear it. "Sophia?" It was Annabella. She knocked again. "Sophia, are you okay?" She tried to open the door. "Let me in, Sophia, please."

I slid away from the door, my back against the cabinet under the sink instead. Annabella opened the door just wide enough for herself to squeeze through. "Soph, what's wrong?"

I shook my head.

Annabella sat down beside me, pulling me into her arms. It took every ounce of strength in my body to not sob harder. "Baby, talk to me. What's wrong?" she asked quietly, her mouth just inches from my ear. I could feel her breath. "Is it your mom?"

I nodded, unable to speak.

Annabella kissed my head. "I'm so sorry, baby. I really am." She rubbed my back, coaxing out the last few sobs I had energy for. "Some people are just hateful. You don't need her, Sophia. I know she's your mom and you love her and I would never tell you that you're wrong for that, but you don't need her." She squeezed me. "You are so beautiful and powerful and I am constantly in awe of you, Sophia. You don't need her. You don't need me. You don't need anyone."

I shook my head feebly.

"That's what you told me, remember? When I was upset about Aliyah?" Annabella's voice was level and cool. "You told me that I didn't need anyone. And you were right. And you don't need anyone, either. Life isn't about needing people. You're strong on your own. Sometimes you're even stronger without them."

I didn't make a sound. I didn't move. I didn't even breathe.

"All you need is you. You're okay, baby. You're okay." Annabella brushed my damp hair away from my face, gently tucking it behind my ear. I wanted to scream. She resumed rubbing my back, watching me carefully.

I closed my eyes.

"You're okay, Sophia."

I didn't respond.

"Say it."

I shook my head.

"Sophia baby, you have to say it. You won't be able to get up until you say it. We'll live and die here on this bathroom floor together if you don't say it." Nothing. "Humor me, alright? Tell yourself you're okay." I couldn't do it. "Tell me you're okay."

"I'm okay." I said.

"You're okay." Annabella repeated. "You were okay before, you're okay now, and tomorrow you will be okay still. And you'll always be okay. Sometimes even better than okay."

"What if I'm not?"

"That's okay," she said. "I'm not saying you'll never be not okay, baby, but you just have to know that it'll pass and you will be okay again. It's okay to cry on the bathroom floor sometimes, but you have to tell yourself you're okay and get back up eventually."

"You made me say it. What if I'm not ready to get back up?" My throat burned.

Annabella kissed the side of my head. "Then I'll stay here with you until you are, as long as you promise me you'll get up eventually," she said, running her hands through my hair.

"You don't have to stay. I'll be okay."

Annabella laughed. "I know you will be. But there's nowhere else I'd rather be."

I closed my eyes again.

I managed to get off of the bathroom floor maybe an hour or so after that. Annabella's sisters and Moms had gone to bed while we were in there, and the house was quiet. In her room, we stripped off our jeans in silence, then crawled into her bed. We curled around each other, a pair of parenthesis, and I let my fingers trace shapes on the slice of skin between her underwear and her t-shirt.

I caught myself thinking that I wouldn't mind falling asleep with her every night for the rest of my life.

I woke up the next morning to a sudden chill and an empty space where Annabella had been. My eyes opened just in time to see the bedroom door shut. I rolled onto my back and stared up at the ceiling, pulling the blankets around myself.

My eyes drifted closed for what felt like only a second, but must have been several minutes. When they opened again, Annabella was climbing into bed again with two plates of food. "Good morning," she said. "I made you breakfast." I sat up and took the plate of eggs and toast from her.

"Thank you, that was sweet of you."

Annabella grinned. "I know, I'm great." She laughed. "And cute and hilarious and fun to be around."

I laughed, too. "And humble."

"So humble," she said solemnly. "Humble to the point of self-depreciating, in fact. I should probably work on that. Start owning my amazing accomplishments. Start loving my beautiful sexy funny amazing self."

"You really should. This humbleness is bordering on self-loathing. I'm truly worried about you."

Annabella laughed again, something about the sound reminded me of tiny pink bubbles. Each note in her laugh was another bubble bursting in the air. I found myself overwhelmed with the desire to lean over and kiss her, but I restrained myself.

She pulled the blanket over her legs, then draped her legs over mine. She ate her eggs in silence with her head on my shoulder, even though the angle appeared to make it harder for her. I spent more time watching her eat than I did actually eating. I never got tired of watching her, of looking at her. She was exquisite.

My heart felt like it was swollen.

"What are you thinking about?" Annabella asked.

"You."

She kissed me on the cheek. My chest fluttered. "Stop it," she said. "You're so cute."

"What are you thinking about?"

Annabella hesitated. "Nothing, really. You. Me. Us."

"Us?"

Annabella shrugged, lifting her head off my shoulder. "It's nothing." She kissed me on the cheek. "Don't worry. Eat up, I've got big plans for today." She took her unfinished plate and got out of bed, disappearing into the hallway. Something inside me cracked in half, leaving a weird empty space.

Her "big plans" consisted mainly of hanging around her house for most of the morning and part of the afternoon, until about three o'clock. We lounged on the couch with our legs draped over each other and didn't talk about much of anything. Something about the lazy easiness settled the wild animal in my ribcage. I only thought about my mother once, and I quickly shoved the intrusive thought away. I didn't need it. I didn't need her.

I'm okay.

When we finally did depart, Annabella took me to a nearby dog park. I wasn't sure if I had ever mentioned to her how much I loved dogs or if she was just a good guesser, but either way I was beyond ecstatic. I hadn't had a dog since my dad died and my mom gave ours away.

Annabella brought her dog, a huge chocolate lab named Lucy. The entire time we were in the car, she at on my lap, crushing me, moping and crying. I stroked her head and promised her that we would be there soon and that she would have lots of other dogs to play with. If she understood me, she showed no sign of it, and continued crying pathetically until she finally got out of the car.

I opened the door slowly, ignoring the spike of pain as Lucy jumped off of my lap. She stretched her legs in the sun, perking up instantly. I got out of the car to join her, stretching myself as well. Her thick brown tail wacked against my legs rhythmically as Annabella clipped on her leash.

We didn't talk much while we were there, except to Lucy and the other dogs, that is. But I could feel her eyes on me when I turned away from her. Her gaze drifting away and back to me every minute or two. I pretended not to notice it. I was careful not to look back at her. But I still couldn't stop smiling.

It was amazing to me that she thought I was something worth looking at. Something she couldn't take her eyes off of. Something beautiful.

I wondered if I was being vain and imagining it. But when I finally caved and looked over at Annabella, I caught her looking at me, too. She laughed and turned back to the dog she was petting.

We went back to her house after that to drop off Lucy and change for dinner. I'd made the mistake of drunkenly telling her the night before that I had never been on a proper date, and she had decided that it was her job to take me on one.

Well, maybe it wasn't that much of a mistake.

"What do I wear?" I asked. I didn't want to over or under dress. I was so nervous. My heartbeat was migrating up into my throat, but I tried my best to swallow it down. I didn't need to be anxious. I was happy. I was safe.

Annabella shrugged. "Whatever you want. I'm not concerned," she said. "You look beautiful whatever you wear, baby." There was that word again. Baby. I tried to remember if she had called me that before we became... whatever we were. If she called everyone that. If it meant anything.

"It'd be easier if you just told me where we were going."

Annabella laughed. "But where's the fun in that?" She kissed me on the cheek. "Just wear whatever you're comfortable in, Soph. It's not a big deal."

In the end, I opted for gray-black skinny jeans and a pale blue shirt that made my boobs look nice. That was about as far as my 'dressing up' ability really went. I preferred to be comfortable, and anything more than that made me feel self-conscious.

When I was dressed, I packed up my things (we were driving back to school that night) and I went to the kitchen to wait for Annabella. Her Mom was sitting at the counter reading. She glanced up at me after a moment.

"You look lovely, Sophia," she told me with a smile. "I'm so glad you came and spent some time with us over your spring break." She folded the corner of her page and put the book down. "I hope you come visit again sometime. You're always welcome here, sweetheart."

"Thank you," I said earnestly. "I had a really nice time. It was so good to meet you."

Calliope stood and rounded the counter. She stood across from me, still smiling. "If there's anything you ever need, Sophia, please don't hesitate to ask." She hesitated. "Anna told me about your mom. The same thing happened with my parents. If you ever want to talk, I'm here for you."

"Thank you," I said, looking down. I didn't want her to see the tears I felt burning behind my eyes.

"Can I hug you?" she asked. I nodded. She wrapped her arms around me tightly, pulling me into her. After a second of hesitation, I hugged her back, letting my head rest on her shoulder. It felt like a weight lifted.

Annabella took me to a pretentious-looking vegan restaurant just outside of town. The woman who seated us handed us our menus and told us our waitress would be over in a minute to take our drink orders. I skimmed over the menu. The soup alone was $20.

"We're definitely splitting the bill," I told her.

Annabella laughed and shook her head. "I told you, it's my treat. I'm taking you on a date, Sophia."

"No, it's way too expensive."

"No worries," Annabella said. "I know the waitress." And as if on cue, Cora came to our table to take our orders. "We have to bring her back to school with us once she gets off," Annabella explained. "So I figured we might as well take advantage of her."

Cora rolled her eyes and turned to leave. "Keep it up, maybe I won't let you use my discount," she called over her shoulder.

"Sophia," Annabella said after taking a sip of her water. "I can't remember if you ever told me this. Do you believe in God?"

The question caught me off guard. "What?" I shook my head. "No, I guess not. Not really. I don't know. I think about things in terms of her existing sometimes, but I guess I don't really believe. It's like a habit."

"Her?"

I frowned. "What, god can't be a girl?"

"You just said you don't believe in god."

"Well, the god I don't believe in is a woman. I decided that when I was little and did believe in her," I explained. "I think my dad started it, actually. My mom hated it, so did my Sunday school teachers." I laughed a little at the memory. "But no one could ever give me a good enough reason for god to *not* be a woman."

"Fair enough. God isn't real but if she is she's a woman."

"You said you maybe believe in god, right?"

Annabella shrugged. "I more believe than don't nowadays. But I'm open to the possibility that I'm wrong."

"That's a good attitude to have. I wish my mom was more like that," I said, sighing. "Why do you ask, anyway?"

"No reason. Just conversation." Annabella played with her fork. "What about mermaids?"

I laughed. "The ocean is big and we haven't explored all of it. I guess it's possible but I'm not holding my breath."

Annabella reached across the table and touched my hair. "You kinda look like a mermaid. It's the hair. How long it is and the way it waves at the bottom," she told me. "I don't believe in mermaids though, I don't think. But if they're real I hope they stay far, far away from us. I don't want to ever know they exist."

"Why?"

She shrugged. "We'd ruin it. We'd kill them or put them in Sea World or something."

"Optimistic."

"Realistic."

"I guess so."

"What about..." Annabella frowned, searching. "Fate? Destiny? All that corny stuff that shitty romcoms thrive off of?"

"Hey, I like shitty romcoms," I said. "But no, not really. I'd like to think I have control over my life to some degree anyway. And I don't really know who would be controlling... fate or whatever. If there's no God, I mean."

Annabella laughed "I like them too. I agree with you on that." She took another sip of water. "Never liked the idea that there was someone up there pulling the strings. I think if god is real, she probably stays out of most things. Probably just watches, you know? Helps out when she feels like it but mainly just... babysits. Makes sure we don't mess up *too* bad."

"Well how do you account for people who *do* mess up too bad?"

"I meant as a species. The human race."

"We've been known to mess up," I pointed out. "Where was god then?"

Annabella hesitated. "Maybe taking a nap," she laughed. "Or doing something else. Maybe she's got a bunch of planets to keep an eye on. A bunch of realities. She's probably very busy. She can't be watching *all* the time."

I liked how quickly she'd adopted my habit of calling god 'she.' I liked how eager she was to talk about the kinds of things no one ever really did. I liked that she seemed genuinely interested in my answers. I liked talking to her. I liked her.

"That makes sense," I said. "No one can be watching everything all the time. Not even God."

"What do you think she looks like?"

"God?"

"Yeah. I think she's probably Indian. Or maybe Rwandan." Annabella speculated.

"I'm not sure God has any nationality."

"Well, Jesus did, right?" Annabella shrugged. "So like, the next Jesus. Female Jesus. Definitely Indian or Rwandan."

"I can see it. Indian Female Jesus," I agreed. "And she's definitely a huge lesbian, too."

"Oh of course. And deaf."

"Deaf Indian Lesbian Jesus."

"I bet she supports communism," Annabella added. "The first Jesus totally would've anyway. I can't imagine political views change much from Jesus to Jesus." Cora brought our food then, setting the dishes down on the table and disappearing without another word. "Sophia, do you like kids?"

I raised an eyebrow. That was unexpected. "Kids?"

"You know," Annabella said. "Little tiny ones. Small humans. Smaller than me? You know. The new humans." She laughed. "Do you like them?"

I laughed. "Yeah, I love kids. Why? Do you?"

"Love 'em. They're real cute. But they terrify me, to be entirely honest," Annabella said. "I don't know what to do with them. And they need so much. I'm afraid of breaking them."

"They're pretty sturdy," I assured her.

"Maybe so." Annabella took a bite of her food. "But they're still pretty scary."

I laughed. "Well that's not something we'll have to worry about any time soon, anyway." It wasn't until the sentence was out that I realized I'd said 'we.'

If she noticed, she didn't say anything.

seventeen
annabella morgan avery
March 31

Like most nights since meeting Sophia, I
dreamed of her once we parted ways and went to
our respective dorms that night. It was nothing
particularly memorable; I dreamed that we went to
an airport together and woke up while we were
boarding. I was pulled back into reality at three am
in a cold sweat, anxiously reaching for her and
realizing that she wasn't there. When I woke up
enough to open my eyes, realize where I was and
the distance between Sophia and I, something inside
of my chest deflated.

I rolled over and tried to get back to sleep,
but the room was colder now. The hum of the hall
lights, perpetually left on, was louder now. My bed
was bigger now. There was a gnawing feeling in my
gut and I thought about waking August up to talk to
her but I didn't know why. She was too cynical. She
wasn't the dating type. Girls came and went for her,

each meaning less than the one before her. She wouldn't understand, or want to understand, the way every cell in my body was aching for Sophia. How I felt like my hands were made to hold hers. How my mouth was made to kiss hers.

I thought about what Liliana told me, about the Chinese and their threads, and wondered if there was something to that. If there was some invisible thread connecting Sophia and me. If I was doing only harm by stretching it out. I was inexplicably drawn to her, that much was undeniable. What was I fighting against? What was I running from?

Groaning, I rolled into my back and stared up at the ceiling. I let my eyes slide in and out of focus, making the cracks and lines in the tiles dance. I pretended not to think about Sophia. I pretended I wasn't pretending not to think about her. I pretended I didn't realize how absurd it was to pretend when there was no one inside my head but myself. When no one else knew that she was all I could think about. When I wasn't even managing to fool myself.

The muscles in my hand and fingers wanted to reach for my phone and call her right then and tell her how badly I wanted her, but the muscles in my arm told them no. My brain thanked my arm but my heart ached for my hand. I was fighting with myself. And I wasn't sure which side I wanted to win.

A sigh escaped my lips and I pulled my pillow out from under my head, planting it firmly on my face.

I spent my entire 10 am class thinking about Sophia and the way her hair moved in the wind. The way it tangled around her face and got caught on the bridge of her nose and on her eyelashes. I thought about how soft it was, how it really *did* remind me of mermaids. How I wanted to bury my face in it and breathe in the scent of her and hold her for the entirety of the conceivable future.

I spent my entire 12 pm class thinking about the way her laughter made something in me burst. The way each peak in her giggles reminded me of bubbles bursting or flowers blooming or notes on a piano. The way that just hearing it made my heart preform acrobatics in my chest. The way knowing that I had made her laugh made my head float off into space. How I could listen to her laugh for decades and never be bored of it.

By 2 o'clock, all I could think about was the shape and feel of her lips against mine. The way I could taste the minty, cold chapstick she used. The way it made my mouth tingle. The way she scraped her teeth against my bottom lip. The way I couldn't stop myself from laughing every time we kissed. How kissing her made me feel so whole, so complete, so full, that I couldn't control my giggles. How she smiled against my mouth every time I did.

I sat in the dining commons until Sophia got out of class at 4 o'clock. I spent the entire two hours thinking about how perfect she was. How easy she was to be around. How easy it was to talk to her about anything and everything and nothing at all. How amazed I was by her. How amazed I was by how drawn I was to her. I had known this girl for less than a month but everything in me was yearning for her. I felt her name blooming in my mouth and something about it felt like coming home.

I wanted to take her to the movies. Bowling. To greenhouse gardens and New York City and beaches on the west coast. I wanted to bring her to Paris and Cairo and Reykjavik and Prague and Beijing. I wanted to picnic in a turf field at night with her. I wanted to backpack across Europe with her. I wanted to kiss her in every world capital, every rural village, every gas station and grocery store parking lot in America. I wanted to go grocery shopping with her. I wanted to buy laundry detergent together. Wash dishes. Fold the laundry. Do taxes. Send Christmas cards. I wanted everything and anything. The extraordinary and the mundane. All of it. Every second of it.

I wanted her.

When she sat down across from me at ten past four, my breath caught in my chest. My thoughts hadn't done her justice. She was even more beautiful than I remembered. It caught me off guard every time. My memory never served me any real justice. I couldn't keep her beauty in my mind's eye. It was too celestial. Too otherworldly.

"How was class today?" she asked, setting down her wrap and glass of water.

I shrugged. "Nothing exciting. You?" I couldn't have told her what happened in class if I tried. I was too busy thinking about her. Too busy daydreaming. I wondered if she thought about me at all. I wondered what she thought about, period. I wanted to know everything that was going on inside of her. What did she think about when she was alone? What was she afraid of? What did she want more than anything? I could imagine the answers, I knew her well enough, but I wanted to *know*. I wanted her to tell me. I wanted her to want to tell me.

"Yeah, me either." She took a bite of her wrap, then looked back up at me. "Are you alright?" she asked, hand covering her mouth. Her sweater sleeve covered all but the very tips of her fingers.

"Me?" I shook my head, as if waking myself up. I was in a daze. "Yeah, I'm fine. Why?"

Sophia shrugged. "You seem off. Are you sure you're alright?" Her brow furrowed. I realized she was worried about me and warmth spread through my chest. There was something so validating about it. Something so important about knowing another human being cared for you enough to worry. Enough to tell when you were off and worry that you might not be okay. It was small, but it felt huge. Everything with her did.

"Yep. Just distracted. Sorry." I shrugged it off. "I've been thinking a lot lately."

"Don't be," she said, taking a sip of water. "What's on your mind?"

"You."

Sophia looked surprised. "Oh yeah? What about me?" She asked. She looked away from me and started fussing with her hair, running her hands through it. I wanted to take her hand, but I didn't.

"I don't want to talk about it here. When you're done eating we can go for a walk or something." I smiled. In reality, I didn't care about talking about it here. I just hadn't found the right words. And the possibility that she didn't want to be with me had finally occurred to me. I had to make it perfect. I had to find the right words.

I should have been anxious, but I'd never felt more at peace.

It was a beautiful, sunny day, so we decided to sit on the quad and talk. We walked there in silence, my hand dangling painstakingly close to hers. I wondered if I could pinpoint the exact moment that I became so aware of my body and the surrounding space. I didn't recall ever really noticing the distance between myself and someone else unless it was too close. I certainly never dwelled on it like this.

Did I even feel this way when I was falling in love with Zoe? I couldn't remember. But then, I didn't care to.

I sat down cross-legged on the grass. Sophia laid down beside me, resting her head on my thigh. My hands absently wandered to her hair, smoothing it away from her face and gently pulling out the tangles. I caught myself marveling in its softness.

"So what did you want to talk about?" Sophia asked, looking up at me. The butterflies that now made a permanent home in my stomach woke up. I started a tiny braid on the side of her head, letting the rhythmic movement steady my hands.

"Us."

Sophia made a face for a fraction of a second, but I couldn't catch exactly what emotion it was. "What about us?" she asked. I couldn't pinpoint anything from the tone of her voice, either.

I hesitated, my fingers stopping mid braid. "What do you want, Sophia?" I asked. "With us."

"I want you," she told me without hesitation.

My stomach flipped. "I mean more specifically than that. Do you want…?" I choked out a laugh. "I guess what I'm asking, or trying to ask anyway, is do you want to like. Be my girlfriend?" I laughed again, feeling a headache bloom and melt away in seconds. "I had a much better way of asking you in my head. I was going to tell you this thing Liliana told me about this Chinese myth about people being connected to each other with these threads. I was going to say that we haven't known each other for very long but I feel that with you, you know? And I feel like our thread is short and I'm straining myself by trying to be apart from you. Something like that." I shook my head.

Sophia sat up, but she didn't say anything.

"But now I'm saying it and it sounds stupid so maybe I shouldn't have said anything at all and you're not saying anything either and I can't really tell from your face what you're thinking and I'm rambling so please, Sophia, feel free to cut in here and stop me at any time because my mouth is drying up real fast and—" She kissed me. Every wire inside me was snipped all at once and my muscles relaxed. I kissed her back.

Sophia pressed her forehead to mine, our noses brushing. Her breath was sweet and warm on my face. Her hand raised and she brushed my jaw with her thumb. "Yes, Annabella, I want to be your girlfriend." She took my face in her hand and kissed me again. I could feel her smiling against my lips. I kissed her back like the entire world would come to an end if I didn't. Maybe it would have.

We spent the rest of the afternoon together in the grass. That word kept rolling around in my mouth. Girlfriend. It felt heavy and soft and round on my tongue. I fumbled with it at first, even though it hadn't been that long since I'd had a girlfriend. It felt different now. It felt less like part of a whole and more like a unit in and of itself. Rounder. More complete.

When the sun set, it sucked all the warmth with it. Sophia and I stood, brushing tendrils of damp, clinging grass off each other's backs. I took her back to my room then. Neither of us said it, but we didn't want to be apart just yet. In my case, I didn't want to be apart ever. The calla lilies she had planted under my skin were growing towards her sunlight, and so was I.

"I want to kiss you," she said suddenly. We were wrapped up in each other on my bed. The only light in the room came from the Christmas lights around August's side of the room, and the lilac candle that was burning on my desk across the room. Its scent was sweet, but it had nothing on Sophia. The room was warm, but we were cocooned in a blanket together anyway, her head resting on my shoulder.

I smiled, looking down at her. "So kiss me."

Sophia sat up, barely containing her laughter, and pecked me lightly on the cheek. I could feel daisies bloom where her skin met mine. They stretched their long stems and white petals towards her, soaking in her warmth.

I smiled harder, my fingers brushing the daisies on my cheek. "You missed." She leaned in and kissed me on the lips this time, and I laughed into her mouth. Her lips were impossibly soft and sweet. I felt her slide her hand onto my thigh, burning me where her fingers brushed my skin.

Too soon, I pulled away, and still laughing, she pulled me back in, crushing herself against me. I wondered if it was possible to get drunk off a girl's lips. I certainly felt it. Could she taste my smile like I tasted the tiny, sweet bubbles of her laughter? Every part of me was blooming. I was a garden underneath her.

"Sophia?" I asked in between kisses. I'd never heard my voice so soft. "What are you doing later tonight?"

She raised an eyebrow. "Depends. What are you doing later tonight?"

Something in my chest melted. "Well I'd like to be kissing you, preferably."

"Then I guess that's what I'm doing tonight."

"And what about every night after that?"

Sophia kissed me again.

She fell asleep sometime around midnight. I had never seen another person fall asleep so suddenly. One second she was telling me about how she wanted to live in Maine or maybe North Dakota someday, and the next, her eyes slid shut and her breathing leveled.

I reached over her and took my phone off of my nightstand, wanting to check my email before going to bed. I'd been avoiding it for the last couple weeks for whatever reason, and the stress was quickly building up.

I scrolled through a bunch of spam and junk mail for a few seconds before I came to across email from the University of Colorado. I'd applied the morning I broke up with Zoe and then subsequently forgot about it. It was my dream school, but my high school GPA wasn't high enough to get in.

Figuring it was another rejection, I opened the email with my thumb hovering over the tiny trash can in the corner. The school's Wi-Fi was awful and the email was loading so painstakingly slowly that I almost just deleted it without bothering to read it. And then, all at once, the image loaded and something inside of me snapped clean in half.

I got in.

eighteen
sophia jane kalvak
April 1

I didn't get back to my room until after class the next morning. There were crawling fluttering slithering animals bustling in my stomach when I punched in the door code and walked in. Emma was sitting on her bed, reading the same book she always seemed to be reading. It was her favorite, she'd read it at least a dozen times since the start of the school year. I wondered how she could reread it so many times and still look so enthralled every time.

Maybe I should read it sometime.

"Sophia," she said as soon as I walked in. She put the book down on her lap, cracked spine facing up and pages splayed. "What time did you leave this morning? I woke up and you were gone. I must have missed you."

I put my bag down at the foot of my bed. "I didn't come home last night, sorry." My bed creaked as I sat down. "I should've texted you but I forgot." She always texted me when she wasn't going to be home. She knew I worried. I should've given her the same courtesy. But the thought apparently hadn't even crossed her mind.

"You didn't?" Emma raised her eyebrow. "Where were you?" she asked. "Sophia Jane, were you with a *boy* last night?"

I laughed, hard.

Emma laughed too, but she sounded confused. "That was mostly a joke. But really, it's not like you to not come home. Is everything okay?"

I nodded. "Everything's fine. Better than fine, actually." I paused for second, stomach fluttering. "I was with my *girl*friend."

Emma's eyes widened. "Your *girlfriend*?"

"Annabella."

My roommate laughed. "I knew it, I totally knew it. I called it."

"You did."

"Why didn't you *tell me?*" she demanded, throwing her pillow at me. "Sophia! You have a girlfriend and you didn't *tell me!*" I couldn't tell if she was mad or surprised. Her tone was similar in both cases. "That's something I'd want to know about my best friend, don't you think?" Maybe hurt, too.

"I'm sorry, I wanted to tell you. It was just all very. Fast. We kissed at Elise's party and she told me she liked me the next day and I wanted to tell you but then I went home and..." I sighed. "I made the mistake of telling my mom and it was this big whole mess. It wasn't even official until yesterday."

"You told your mom?" Emma's voice dropped instantly. "Dude, what happened?"

My eyes stung, but remained dry. "She kicked me out. I stayed with my Nana. It's... fine. It's whatever. I wanted to call you but I couldn't, like, talk about it. But it's okay," I said. "I don't need her. I'm okay."

Emma got up and crossed the room to my bed. She sat down next to me, arm around my waist. "I'm sorry, dude, I had no idea." She kissed my temple. "You're right though. You don't need her. You're okay."

"I know."

"I can't believe you have a *girlfriend*." Emma sat up, shaking her head. "Are you like, full lesbian, or?" I half shrugged, half nodded. I hadn't given the label much thought, but I figured I was. Kissing girls was infinitely better than kissing boys. Everything I had always been missing was there. No part of me ever wanted to kiss or be with a boy. "Sorry if that's weird to ask."

"It's not weird," I assured her. "Don't worry about it."

Emma was quiet for a long time. "Have you talked to your mom since then?"

I rolled my eyes. "I drunk dialed her. But she didn't answer. I think I left her a message." I snorted. "I don't know. Nana said I can stay with her this summer if I need to."

"It's good that your nana is supportive."

"Yeah, I'm lucky. She ripped my mom a new one, too. When we went back to get my things a couple days later. She threw bible quotes at her and told her that she was ashamed of her," I said. "Did you know that that bible verse about like, 'where you go I will follow, your people will be my people' yadda yadda, was from one woman to another?" I asked. "Like, I know so many straight people who use that in their vows. My mom did."

"There are lesbians in the bible?" Emma asked.

I shrugged. "I guess so. Or maybe they're bisexual. I don't know, it's been a long time since I read the bible. But my nana said that Ruth and Naomi were in love. Even if that's not a hundred percent true, I'd like to believe it anyway." I frowned. "It's nice to think that there are people like me in the bible, even if I don't believe it. And it's nice to imagine homophobes using the words of a lesbian to ascertain their love for each other." Emma laughed.

I caught myself wishing my dad was alive to mellow my mom out. He was always more relaxed, more accepting. She hadn't gotten so heavily into religion until after he died, either. Maybe if he was alive things would've been different. Maybe she would've been less homophobic to begin with. Or maybe he would've comforted her and calmed her down and protected me. His favorite piece of folklore *was* about a lesbian sea goddess.

He would still love me. I knew he would.

But there was no real point in wishing for that. He was gone, he'd been gone, and I was, for the most part, over it and okay.

I didn't want to dwell on it anymore. All thinking about it was doing was hurting me. And I'd had enough of that. I wanted to be happy. I deserved to be happy. I was happy.

I had never been anyone's girlfriend before. Besides the obvious aversions and misunderstandings of my own desires, there was something fundamentally unappealing about it to me. There was the subservient relationship between husband and wife that Catholicism lauded, of course, but I never really ascribed to that. Not on a conscious level, anyway. It wasn't the concept of submitting, it was the idea of belonging to another person. Because even if you didn't submit, even if you weren't cleaving to your significant other, there was still a sense that you belonged to them, and them to you.

I never liked that. I was not an object to belong to someone. I was not a gift to pass from my family to my Future WASP Husband—or anyone. I wasn't a restless person, I was perfectly content to be where I was, wherever that was, but that didn't make me a home.

Through a series of not so great friends I'd had when I was younger and semi-depressed, I'd developed this chronic fear of being seen as a project. A fixer upper. A place to make a home out of but not for yourself. Something, not someone, who had kinks to smooth out and broken shutters to repair and a roof that needed re-shingling. Something to make livable and lovable for someone else. And when they thought they had fixed whatever issue they saw with me, or when my stubbornness cause them to quit, they vanished. Leaving me with shitty memories, a half shingled roof, and a complex I couldn't shake.

I was not a home, or at the very least, not a very good one. But I could be, for Annabella. I wanted to be a home for her. I wanted to carve out a space between my ribs for her. Maybe you shouldn't make homes out of people, but if anyone was going to, I wanted it to be her.

There was just something about her. Something that felt like safety. I didn't mind where I was or where I ended up, as long as Annabella was there with me. She could make a home in me any time she liked.

Annabella and I spent the day walking through campus, pointing out the freshly planted and newly bloomed flowers. Daffodils, tulips, daisies, and pansies. She made a joke of naming each almost-blossomed head.

"Christopher, Michaela, Angela, Cassie," she introduced them to me. "Andrew, Meghan, Lucy, Alexandra." One hand pointed each named flower, the other held mine tightly.

"You're ridiculous," I told her, laughing. "Who names flowers?"

"Exactly," she said. "Someone has to do it."

"Maria, Javier, Edna, Avni, Li."

Annabella laughed. "See, doesn't it feel nice to name them?"

I kissed her on the cheek. "It does. You were right."

"I'm always right," she told me with a wink. I laughed.

That night, I decided to call my mother again. I knew I shouldn't. I knew it would only hurt me. I knew that no amount of calling or crying or screaming could make her into the person I wanted her to be. But she was my mom. Some part of me still felt this chronic need to please her, to include her, to feel love from her.

I went to the lounge on the third floor of my building to call her, hoping that no one else would be up there. Luckily, it was empty, as it always seemed to be. I sat on a couch in the far corner, pulling my knees up to my chest. I messed around on my phone for a couple minutes, pretending that I wasn't putting it off.

When I finally mustered up the courage to call her, my heart was already in the back of my mouth. If I opened my mouth too widely, it would fall out onto the ugly, dusty carpet. I wasn't sure that that was necessarily the worst possible outcome to this phone call. Regardless, I tried not to open my mouth too wide.

The phone rang and rang and rang and my heart fell down into the pit of my stomach, sinking deeper into my pelvis with each ring.

The line picked up. I could hear a TV in the background for a moment, until it was cut off suddenly. She didn't say anything.

"Mom?"

Nothing. But she didn't hang up, either. The silence of her end of the line caused a sort of static in my phone. The absence of noise was louder than anything she could've said.

"Mom, it's me. It's Sophia." She had caller ID, of course. She knew it was me. She knew it was me, and she picked up the phone. Or maybe she'd accidentally answered. She still wasn't saying anything. My heart jumped up into my throat but I swallowed it down, keeping it suspended in my chest where it was supposed to be. Somehow that still felt like limbo.

"I just wanted to tell you that I'm still not sorry. I mean, I'm sorry for calling you the other night. I'm kind of sorry for calling you now," I admitted. "I know you don't want to talk to me and I know I should be an adult and respect that. But you should be an adult and respect *me*." Something in my throat caught on fire. "I want you to know that I don't need you."

Nothing.

"I don't need you, Mom. I'd like for you to grow up and love me again and meet my girlfriend, but I don't need you to." I paused. "I have a girlfriend, Mom. She's beautiful. And amazing. And I'm happy. And we are not broken."

It sounded like she was crying.

I pretended not to notice. "You don't need to be in my life. I'm an adult and I can get on just fine without you, Mom. And I will, if I have to. You can keep going to Church and hating me and I'll keep being a lesbian and being happy without you." I was trying so hard to keep the fire burning in my throat, because if it didn't, everything would crumble. "You can be hateful all you want. But don't kid yourself into thinking it's godly."

She was definitely crying.

"Dad would have wanted you to love me." It was low, but I was hurting. The fire was dying out. "Nana wants you to love me. I'm sure god wants you to love me. She wouldn't want you to turn your back on me because of how she made me. But if you want to, that's your prerogative. I can't stop you. I don't want to stop you." I felt my voice crack, but I pretended it didn't. "I don't want to force you to love me or be in my life. I want you to want to."

Silence.

"I'm happy, Mom. She makes me happy. And you're not going to ruin that."

Nothing.

"You can say something now. Otherwise I'm going to hang up and I'm not going to call you again."

I heard shuffling in the background, but no words. Just her broken-sounding breathing. An unsteady in-and-out that assured me that she was there, she was listening, but she didn't love me enough to speak. Why was she even on the line? What was she possibly getting out of this?

"That's what you want, then?" I sighed, feeling defeated and low. "Okay. Fine. You can call me when you're feeling up to being a mother again. Otherwise, this is it. I'm not going to call you. I'm not going to write to you. I'm not going to even think about you. Because you don't deserve it."

There was an intake of breath, almost like she was going to speak. I waited. She exhaled.

I ended the call.

I rested my head on the back of the couch, staring up at the high, tilted ceiling. My throat was burning again but it wasn't the same. It spread down to my chest and stomach and limbs and I felt like I was being submerged in warm water. I felt strong. I felt important. I felt in control. I felt like she couldn't hurt me anymore.

My phone buzzed and I looked down to see that it wasn't her calling me back, and I felt nothing. I didn't care. I didn't need her. I was going to be whole and happy with or without her.

I laid my head back on the couch again and marveled in the fact that my eyes were dry. There were no knots in my throat or chest. My heart was carrying on steadily in my chest, *ga-dump, ga-dump, ga-dump*. I thought about her, sitting alone on the couch, crying and probably clutching her rosary beads. I thought about her church group praying for my soul. I thought about her voting for candidates that undermined my humanity. I thought about her thinking that I was evil and broken and sinful.

I didn't feel any of those things. I felt whole. She could believe I was anything she wanted to. None of the words she could come up with could undermine my wholeness.

My eyes remained dry.
I did not cry.

nineteen

annabella morgan avery
April 2

Cora looked at me incredulously. "Wait, you and Sophia are dating now?" she asked. "When did that happen? Why didn't you tell me, Anna?" She looked mildly hurt, but I couldn't really bring myself to care. A small forest fire started in my stomach and spread to my arms. My muscles tensed. She was missing the point. She was entirely missing the point.

"Yes. We're dating now. She is my girlfriend," I said shortly. "Which is amazing and I am so so happy and so so lucky except I *got into UCB*." No matter how many times I said it, it still didn't feel real. Neither statement, I mean. They both seemed too good to be true. And I guess, in a way, they were. I wanted to be with Sophia so badly that every bone in my body ached, but Colorado was my dream school. I wanted to be there, too. I couldn't have both, could I?

When I was younger, Mom told me a story about a dog who had a bone. He wandered down to a stream with his bone one day and saw his reflection in the water, but confused it for another dog with another bone. Naturally, the dog wanted both bones, and opened his mouth to grab the other out of the water. In the process, he lost his real bone, and wound up with nothing.

I was starting to feel like the dog in the story. Reaching for something that didn't even exist because I wasn't content enough with what I had.

"I don't know what to tell you, kid."

"You're my big sister, you're supposed to know." I felt like a toddler. I wanted to throw a tantrum. I wanted to undo everything in my life that lead me to this impasse. I wanted to go back in time and have gotten into UCB the first time around, and for Sophia to have gone there too. I didn't want to choose between the girl and the school.

Logic said the school. My heart said the girl. Everything in me said *why can't I have both?*

Why couldn't I be happy?

"If you leave, you might lose her," Cora said. "Long distance is so hard."

"I know that."

"But if you stay here, you might lose her anyway. You might resent her for making you stay. For missing out on your dream school," Cora said. "Colorado is a great school. This is a great opportunity."

"Are you saying go?"

"I'm saying you need to do what's best for you, not what's best for her. But I don't know what that is. I honestly don't. I like Sophia, I really do. And I like how happy she makes you." Cora sighed. "I'm sorry, kid, I really don't know what to tell you here."

"All I can think about is everything that could go wrong with either option," I said. "Neither sounds ideal. I want both."

"You can't have both, babe. You can't be physically with her here in New Hampshire and be physically in Colorado. I'm sorry to break it to you.'

"I know that." I put my head on my big sister's lap, trying to pretend I didn't feel all of the pieces inside me shattering. "This isn't fair."

"Life isn't fair."

"I just want to be happy."

"You will be."

When I left Char's, I immediately called Liliana and filled her in. I knew part of me should feel stupid for running to my baby sister for help, but she was often the best help I ever received. And I didn't know what else to do. I wasn't ready to talk to Moms. I wasn't ready to talk to Sophia. I wasn't sure I would ever be ready to talk to Sophia. I was afraid.

Liliana listened to me patiently, though I was sure she thought I was being foolish. She usually did. My little sister had the same advice for me that that she always did.

"Get out of your own head, Anna. Stop thinking about the negative. Think about the positives. You could go to Colorado and things could work. Tons of people have long distance relationships. And yours would only be super long distance for eight months out of the year. You'd be home the other four. Only two hours from her. That's not bad."

"Not bad isn't good enough. I want to be with her, Lil."

"Then be with her. Stay here. You like the school you're at now, anyway. You're close to home. You're capital A Adjusted. You're capital H Happy. Capital I-L In Love," Liliana said. "What can you have at Colorado that you can't have there?"

"They have one of the best psych programs," I said. "I want the best education I can get. I want to do well. I want to succeed. I want to be able to help people someday."

Liliana laughed at me. The sound cut me somewhere deep. "Babe, you can't even help yourself. You need to work on that first."

"That's really mean."

"I love you, Anna, I really do. But Cora is right. We can't give you answers here. It's on you," she said.

"No, you don't get to get out of being mean to me like that. That was a shitty thing to say, Lil. You need to apologize to me. I didn't deserve that."

"Sorry, An. Good on you for sticking up for yourself."

"What do you mean?" I didn't like the way she said it. It made me feel slimy. This whole conversation was making me feel slimy. This whole day was making me feel slimy.

"I just mean, you let people walk all over you. You let *me* walk all over you. It's nice to see you have some backbone for a change. I'm not saying this to be mean. I'm not saying anything to be mean. I love you. I want you to stand up for yourself. I want you to make your own decisions."

I heard what she was saying, but my brain was stuck elsewhere. "I don't want to hurt Sophia."

"I know that," Liliana said, sounding old and tired. "But *I* don't want you to hurt yourself. You need to put Annabella first, not Sophia. If she cares about you, and I really think she does, she'll want that too."

"But what if she doesn't?"

"Then you leave. Colorado doesn't give you ultimatums. I know you think you're in love with this girl, Anna, but if you can't care about yourself, you can't care about anyone. Putting everyone before you isn't love. It's suicide. If she cares you, she'll let you decide on your own," Lil said. "And Anna, please try to remember that you have only known this girl for a month. You are not in love. You are not married. You have no obligation to stay with her forever. Things can change. You can get over her if you need to. You were a whole person before her and you will be a whole person after her."

"You're the one saying I'm in love with her, Lil, not me. I know that I'm not. I just could be. Someday."

"And I could be a Catholic housewife and mother of nine someday," Lil said dryly, "That doesn't mean I should start living my life accordingly now."

I frowned. "You're real dumb for someone who's so smart. That's not similar."

"Okay, fine, I could fall in love with the next boy or girl that I see on the bus. Should I stop my entire life and live it in a way that would foster and nurture that love that *doesn't even exist yet*?"

"No, but…"

"Just do what's best for you, Annabella. Whatever happens happens. You'll be okay. You'll both be okay."

"I don't want to leave her."

"Then *don't*. I'm not telling you to go, I'm telling you to make the choice on your own. I'm telling you to do what you want, not what she wants."

"What if what I want is to make her happy?"

Liliana snorted. "What a small goal. Anyone can make someone else happy. You should want to make yourself happy."

"She makes me happy."

"We're going in circles here, Annabella. I can't help you," my little sister sounded tired again. "I wish I could. I really do. But I can't. And honestly, that's probably for the best. This is all on you."

"I know, I know, I know."

"You're smart, despite the dumb shit you do sometimes," Liliana laughed. "Not as smart as me, but we can't all be perfect. Anyway, I know you'll figure this out on your own. I know you'll make the right choice for you. Even if you don't know what it is right now." I started chewing on my fingernails. "I have faith in you."

"Thanks, Lil."

"No problem. I'll support you no matter what choice you make."

"Even if you think it's stupid or that I made it for the wrong reasons?" I asked, feeling vulnerable and small.

Liliana laughed. "Of course I will. You may be an idiot, but you're my idiot big sister. I'll always love you and support you, Annabella."

"Thanks. I needed to hear that." I laid down and rested the phone on my face. The three blankets I had over myself weren't cutting it. I just couldn't manage to get warm for whatever reason. It was like my bones were made entirely of ice.

"I know you did."

"I love you, Liliana." I smiled. "Sorry for being such a baby. You should've been the big sister. I'm no good at it," I told her.

"Nah, you're good at it. But you were a little sister first. So it's understandable," Liliana said. "Like I said, we can't all be perfect like I am."

I snorted. "You are so conceited. How does your ego even fit in that little head of yours?"

"You let me get this way," Liliana laughed. "All that praise. This is your fault," she said. "I can't and won't be held accountable."

"Right. And that's not a flaw at all."

Liliana laughed again. "Nope. I don't have any of those. Sorry to disappoint."

"You could never."

"I know."

When I saw Sophia later that night, I tried to put all thoughts of Colorado out of my mind. I wasn't going to talk to her about it yet, even if she pressed me on the subject, so it was better to not think about it all together. Better to act as normal as I could. Better to just enjoy my time with her.

In truth, it was easier to forget about than I anticipated.

Sophia and I decided to go to August's poetry reading that night. It was run by some club she wasn't a part of, taking place in a much unused room in the student center. The room was empty when we first arrived, and we took our seats at the table closest to the stage. As time progressed, people slowly filtered in until the room was full. Four strangers took the other seats at our table, kindly introducing themselves one by one. By the time I heard the next name, the one before it had already escaped out of my other ear.

I pulled my chair in close and looked down at the black plastic table cloth, while Sophia played with one of the fake tea lights on a dish in front of us. The table was covered in shiny silver stars. I pressed my index finger against one until it stuck, and then reached over and stuck it on Sophia's nose. It held for a second, then fluttered back down to the table. She laughed, and I leaned over to kiss her nose where the star once was.

The music stopped playing and the lights dimmed. The flickering plastic tea lights added *something* to the atmosphere, but I couldn't say if it was a net win or not.

I felt her leg brush against mine underneath the table. I hadn't realized how cold I was until we were no longer touching. I shifted so that my leg was pressed against hers again. Sophia glanced over at me and smiled. I had butterflies.

The first poet went on, a tall, wiry Asian man that I recognized as Zoe's RA. I couldn't for the life of me remember his name, and even after he introduced himself, it didn't stick. Sophia picked up a star and put it on my nose. It stuck. She turned away to watch the man preform his poem and I tried to, too, but I couldn't stop looking at her.

God, she was so beautiful.

People were clapping, I realized. Sophia turned back to me and I quickly dropped my gaze, but I wasn't sure why. I didn't need to pretend I wasn't looking at her anymore. I looked back up at her, and she was still looking at me. She held my gaze and everything in me sparked up. I reached for her hand but didn't hold it. Instead, I played with her fingers, tracing shapes on her knuckles and moving them around. Sophia laughed again. I thought about how many laughs I would miss out on if I moved to Colorado.

I took the word, folded it up, and threw it into the back of my mind. I wasn't thinking about

Colorado right now. I didn't need to. I was with Sophia.

Thinking about Colorado felt like cheating.

The star fell off my nose, finally. Sophia picked it up and started bending it between her fingers. It shot out, flying at me and fluttering to my lap. I snorted. Someone shushed me, even though no one was speaking yet. Sophia sipped her water innocuously, concealing a smile.

The next poet was a woman I met once or twice my freshman year, back when I thought going to Pride was a good idea. Needless to say, it wasn't. They were weird, and not the kind of weird I was into. I wondered what the intersection rate for Pride and the Anime Club was. She recited a poem she wrote about her mother not accepting her for being a lesbian.

I glanced over at Sophia, whose face was turned away from me. She turned around the moment I looked at her, as if she felt my stare. I smiled at her and she smiled back, taking her fingers out of mine and squeezing my hand. She was okay. I smiled again.

After the lesbian from Pride finished, it was August's turn. I actually turned away from Sophia to give my roommate my full attention. I knew she wrote poetry, but I had never heard nor read any of it before. It felt like a privilege to finally be able to hear it. I couldn't imagine what she wrote about. She always seemed so... emotionally distant.

She was the first to read her poems from a crumpled up piece of paper, but that added to it somehow. August talked about being in love, to my surprise, and having her heart broken. It wasn't anything that particularly resonated with me, but the emotion in her voice nearly brought tears to my eyes. I'd never heard her sound like that. I'd never seen her feel so much. I should have suspected from the get go that there was a reason for the parade of women who flickered in and out of her life. A reason for the variety. A reason for the ceaselessness.

When she sat back down beside me, I took her hand and squeezed it. "You did great, I had no idea you could write like that."

August smiled at me, but pulled her hand out of mine. In the heat of the moment I forgot how much she hated being touched. I mouthed 'I'm sorry' but she shook her head. She was still smiling.

I touched my foot to Sophia's and she tapped my foot back. We played with our feet like that through the next two poets, and I marveled in how something so simple as touching under the table where no one else could see could feel so intimate.

twenty
sophia jane kalvak
April 4

Emma invited Annabella and me to another
party that weekend. I wasn't sure if I wanted to go,
but Annabella convinced me. That band Emma
liked was playing again. August was going to come.
It would be fun, she said. We would have fun.

And it was, for a while. We drank rum from
a plastic handle and danced in a sweaty, smelly
basement. Annabella pressed herself against me in
the heat and the haze of the music and the rum and
kissed me so many times that I lost count. The mass
of damp, heavy, jumping bodies around us slowed
down to a slow wave every time she pressed her lips
to my nose, my mouth, my neck, my collarbones. It
seemed too good to be true. She was too good to be
true. I planted my hands on her waist and held her

to me, anchoring myself in the sea of bodies. Even over the roar of the music, I could hear her laughter floating up to the ceiling. The bass boomed in my chest and I was amazed at how alive it made me feel. How it kick started my heartbeat into overdrive.

Or, maybe that was Annabella.

When the set ended, we filtered back upstairs with the crowd and managed to station ourselves on the couch. Emma sat on one side of me, Annabella on the other. I took a long drink from the plastic handle of rum and tried not to gag at the sweetness. When I was finished, I handed it off to Annabella, telling her not to let me have any more.

The crowd simmered down a bit now that the music was done. Most people left or went outside to smoke or talk or whatever it was drunk people did outside on chilly April nights. The faces most familiar to me hovered in the living room, perching on couches and chairs and leaning up against the wall.

Someone brought a laptop from upstairs and hooked it up to the speakers. They played 2005-2010 era pop punk, much to the delight of the Former Emo Kids Emma seemed to be friends with. My mom never let me listen to the music, but I'd heard it with Emma and at other parties. Even if I didn't know the words well enough to belt them out like everyone else did, I could still nod along and sing the choruses.

Not knowing the words did, however, give me time to look around the room and soak it all in. There was something about seeing so many people so happy, so enthusiastic, that made me feel like I was going to burst. Maybe it was the rum or maybe it was Annabella's arm around my shoulder as she screamed the lyrics to some bad emo song, but I never felt so happy to be alive.

Time passed in three minute chunks, song to song, angsty lyric to angsty lyric. I traced small patterns on the soft skin of Annabella's thigh, once again amazed at how soft she felt. After a minute or two of this, she caught my hand and entwined her fingers with mine. When she kissed me, time stopped.

The music carried on when we broke apart, cautious to not cause a scene. I was admiring the awful pattern on the couch across us when I felt Annabella go stiff beside me. She clasped my hand tightly. I looked up to follow her gaze across the room to a tall, thin blonde girl. The girl looked like she was going to scream.

"I'll be right back," Annabella stood up, dropping my hand, and left the room. I watched her go, feeling cold.

Emma nudged me. "What's that about?" I watched my girlfriend say something to the blonde girl, who followed her out of the house. "Do you know that girl?"

I shook my head. "I've never seen her before."

"Is that her ex?"

I looked over to August, who had been sitting on Annabella's other side. "Was that Zoe who Annabella just walked out with?"

August shrugged. "Didn't see. What'd she look like?"

"Tall. White. Blonde. Thin."

"You just described almost every girl in the great state of New Hampshire, but Zoe does fit the aforementioned description," August said, laughing. "Does she usually come to these things?"

I shook my head. "Not that I know of. I've never seen her before." August frowned. "Do you think Annabella is okay? Should I go out there?"

She shrugged. "The fuck if I know, dude," she said, then grimaced. "Sorry. But, uh, Annabella's probably got it under control. Did Zoe look pissed?" I nodded. August made another face. "Maybe... I'll go check on them, okay? You stay here, kid." She stood up. "Zoe is psychotic. You being out there will only exasperate her. I mean, it's probably fine," she said, looking behind her. "But I'll check."

It didn't seem fine. But I waited. Until I heard them yelling.

"Sophia, August said to wait—" I was already out of the room, halfway through the kitchen, out the front door.

Zoe was in Annabella's face, screaming, and August was standing on the porch uselessly, rambling something to me that I couldn't hear. I pushed past August, sliding out of my sweatshirt when she grabbed onto the sleeve to try to stop me.

Her arms were flailing. It looked like she was going to hit Annabella. Everything inside me froze for a millisecond before bursting into flame. I ran over to them. I could feel my pulse in my eyelids. I wasn't sure I had ever been so angry or so afraid in my entire life.

"Hey!" I shouted, coming up between them. Zoe was still yelling, but I didn't hear words only noises. She was close to Annabella's face. Annabella was crying. Zoe's arms were flailing. "Stop it! Stop it! *STOP IT!*" I pushed them apart, and Zoe's flailing arm caught me under the chin, snapping my head back. I shoved her and she fell on the ground, hard. She was crying now, too.

"Fuck you, Annabella. Fuck you. What the fuck. You told me there was no one else."

Annabella didn't say anything, she just cried harder. Zoe stood up and jerked forward like she was going to push or grab or hit her. I pushed Annabella out of the way and Zoe's hands landed hard on my ribs, shoving me back. I caught myself just in time to keep from toppling backwards onto Annabella.

"And fuck you, too!" Zoe shouted at me. "How dare you, how *dare* you? What the fuck is wrong with you? Who the fuck do you think you are?" She was slurring hard, wobbling as she lurched for me again. I caught her wrists in one hand and held her away from me. "Let go of me! Let *go* of me!"

August finally descended from the porch, as if woken from some sort of daze, and grabbed Zoe from behind, pulling her away from me. She wrapped her arms around her, holding Zoe's arms tight against her waist. She thrashed about for a minute before going limp. She was still crying.

I almost felt bad for her.

"Are you okay?" I asked, turning to my crying girlfriend. The one I really did feel bad for. Annabella nodded, but I pulled her to me anyway. I didn't think I had ever hugged someone so tightly. My heartbeat slowed and I kissed the top of her head. She was shaking. I heard shuffling behind me as August led a now-compliant Zoe inside the house. I didn't know where they were going and I didn't care.

"She thinks I was cheating on her with you."

"Well you weren't, right?"

Annabella shook her head.

I kissed her head again. "She was wrong, then. Shh, don't cry." I squeezed her tighter, if that was possible. She finally wrapped her arms around me. "Are you okay? Did she hurt you?" I pulled back enough to see her face under the dim porch light. Beyond the snot and the tears, I didn't see anything wrong with her. No blood. No swelling. No anything.

"She slapped me." I felt something in me flare up. "Don't worry about it. Really. Don't. She's gone." Annabella looked past me, towards the porch. "Where did August go?"

"She took her inside. I don't know where to. Should I make sure she's okay?" I didn't want to leave Annabella, but I didn't want her to be the one to check on August. She nodded limply. "Okay. Stay right here, okay? I'll be fast. I'll get August and we'll all go home, okay?" She nodded again. I kissed her forehead and jogged back into the house.

When I didn't immediately see them, I poked my head into the living room. "Emma, did you see where August and Zoe went?" I asked, shouting over the music.

"Bathroom?" she called back.

I darted down the hall and knocked on the door. "Occupied!" August called from inside.

"It's Sophia."

"I said occupied."

"Annabella wants me to check on you," I said back, pressing my ear to the door. "Are you with Zoe?" I heard vomiting.

"Yes, I'm with Zoe. You two go home. I've got it covered. Tell her I'm okay. Shit—in the toilet, Zoe, not the floor." She sounded exhausted. I couldn't fathom why she was holding the hair of the girl who had just assaulted her friend, but I didn't care enough to ask.

"Fine, okay, bye."

"Later."

I pushed through the dwindling but somehow still solid crowd of people to get back outside, feeling a thousand times more sober than I had been a few minutes ago. When I got outside, Annabella was sitting up against the house. Her head was on her knees. I knelt down beside her.

"Are you okay, baby?"

She looked up at me. "I'm okay. Where's August?"

"She said for us to go. She's with Zoe."

Annabella looked confused. "She's with Zoe?"

"In the bathroom. Zoe's throwing up. I don't know what they're doing or why she's with her. She said to tell you she's got it covered and that she's okay," I said. I felt weird about the whole thing, but I was uncomfortable pressing it further. I stood up and offered Annabella my hand. She took it, but not eagerly. "Let's just go home, okay? August's fine." I hugged her briefly, then interlocked arms with her.

"Okay. Okay. Let's go." Annabella sniffed. "I'm so sorry about all this."

"Don't be sorry, baby."

"I am."

I kissed her forehead. "Let's go home. Let's get you into bed."

"Will you stay with me?"

"Of course I will, Annabella. I'll stay as long as you want." I squeezed her hand. She squeezed back.

"I want you to stay forever."

I felt something inside of me warm up. Slowly. Like one of those energy efficient light bulbs. The light grew brighter and brighter and despite everything, I smiled. "Then I'll stay forever, baby."

She started crying again.

I made Annabella hot chocolate in the tiny kitchen on her floor. When it was done, I set it on her dresser next to the bed and sat down beside her. She was still shaking, but less than before. I wasn't sure what shock looked like, but I thought it was possible that she was in it. I helped her up off of her bed and undressed her slowly. I wasn't sure if warmer clothes or body heat would help her more, but before I could decide and rifle through her drawers, she was peeling off my layers.

I wasn't sure what she was doing. My sweatshirt and t-shirt fell to the floor with soft *whooshes*. She stood in front of me in her underwear, hands shaking. My hands fumbled in front of me for a minute before taking her wrists and stopping her from unbuttoning my jeans. She kissed me sloppily, and I felt her tears on my face.

"No, Annabella." It finally hit me that she thought I was trying to have sex with her. That, despite all her crying and shaking, she was clearly still drunk and not comprehending what was happening. "I'm just trying to get you warm. I'm just trying to take care of you." She started crying again.

I took her in my arms and led her to the bed. She seemed to crumble into it, only remaining upright because of the wall behind her. I wrapped a blanket around both of our shoulders and pulled her legs over mine. She laid her head down on my shoulder and cried. I didn't know what to do besides run one hand through her hair, lips pressed to her forehead, and hold her hand.

I wanted to ask her if Zoe had ever hit her like that before. I wanted to know why Annabella, who didn't seem like she was afraid of anything, was so afraid of this lithe, elven girl. Why she let her talk to her the way she did. I wanted to know why August, who didn't seem to care about anything, got worried about Annabella being outside with Zoe. Why she froze up on the porch. Why she held Zoe's hair while she vomited in the bathroom after. There was some strange dynamic going on that I didn't think I would ever really understand.

I pushed it all back. None of it mattered right now. What mattered was the fact that my girlfriend was hurting. She was crying and hurting and I needed to be there for her. So I ignored every question I had floating in my head and turned my full attention to her. I told her in muted tones how beautiful and strong and loved she was. I told her I was here for her and I always would be. I said her name, over and over and over.

My phone rang on her dresser and I looked over to see "MOM" on the screen, but no part of me wanted to answer it. It didn't matter that she was calling me. All that mattered was in my arms right now.

Annabella, Annabella, Annabella.

Her name blossomed in my mouth and it tasted like spring. I held her and I realized that I never wanted to be apart from her. I never wanted to stop blooming.

twenty one
annabella morgan avery
April 8

Everything with Zoe seemed to blow over almost overnight. August didn't want to tell me what happened in the bathroom after we left. I didn't remember much about the actual confrontation, and what I did remember, I didn't want to talk about. I didn't want to talk about her hitting me. I didn't want to talk about how it happened once or twice before. I didn't want to talk about Zoe. I wanted it not to exist.

Sophia, luckily, didn't push it. And thankfully, she only looked at me like I was a wounded animal for the next twenty four hours.

After that, we seemed to pretend it didn't happen. Which was what I needed. I needed normalcy. I needed to be human. I needed to forget about Zoe.

No, that seemed cruel. I didn't want to forget about her. I loved her, once. I didn't regret it. I didn't regret her. But I needed to move past it.

I *was* past it. Past her. Her confronting me only solidified that.

I was weirdly glad that it had happened. It felt like the resolution Zoe and I never had. The final blow out to end it. The final realization of why I had actually broken up with her to begin with. She was volatile. She was aggressive. She was bad for me. All the things people had told me but I never listened. I finally got it.

It felt settled. Whatever that meant.

I threw myself into my relationship with Sophia so thoroughly over the next few days that it was easy to forget about Colorado. Except when I wasn't with her. When I was in class, walking through campus, at the dining commons, at the student center. Then, it was hard to forget. It was hard to think about anything but my dream school. The school in the state two thousand miles away.

If lumps formed in my throat often enough, would they stick?

I finally called Moms to tell them that I got into UCB. I'd been meaning to since the day I found out, but somehow, telling them felt like a decision. It felt like I was saying 'yes, this is what I want.' And it was what I wanted. The trouble was that I wanted everything else, too. I was greedy and selfish and childish and weak-willed and indecisive.

"That's amazing, honey!" Ma said.

"We're so proud of you," Mom cooed.

I felt nauseous in some sort of unfamiliar way. My entire body was wracked with it. I felt seasick.

"What about scholarships, did they give you anything substantial? It's a lot more expensive than your school now. Especially since it's out of state."

I swallowed another lump. "Yeah, they did. It'll end up being cheaper, actually."

"Annabella! That's amazing!" Mom exclaimed. I felt dizzy, talking to them both at once. I hated when they put me on speaker phone. They sounded so different in person but so similar through the machine. It gave me headaches.

"Yeah. I'm not sure yet," I told them. But I knew that I was lying. "I have friends here." What I meant was, I had Sophia here. "You guys are here." Sophia was here. "Colorado is my dream school, but that's a lot to leave behind." Sophia was a lot to leave behind.

"Well, we'll support you whatever you choose, of course, but I think it would be silly to stay here," Mom said. I could tell that the idea of me being two thousand miles away made her sad, but she was trying to be supportive. She knew what this meant to me. Apparently more than I did.

"What does Sophia think about this?" Ma asked. Something told me she already knew.

I felt my breath catch. "I haven't told her."

There was silence on their end of the line. I could almost see the looks they were exchanging. "Don't you think you should?" Mom asked quietly. She was so gentle. I appreciated it, but part of me felt like I needed to be yelled at. To be told to tell her. To be ordered to.

"I told you, I haven't made up my mind."

More silence. I wanted to peel off my own skin.

"Well, I think you should tell her sooner rather than later. Even if you haven't decided," Ma said. "But it sounds like you want to go. And I think you should." Her voice lowered. "I know you care about this girl, but you shouldn't risk your future for her."

"What if she is my future?"

"Like your mother said," Ma said with a sigh. "We'll support you no matter what, baby."

Mom interrupted. "You need to tell her."

"I know I do."

"Soon."

"I know, Mom."

"We love you."

"I love you, too."

I couldn't tell her yet, though. I was still trying to convince myself that I hadn't decided. I delved into my savings account and purchased a plane ticket and booked myself a tour of the campus for the next weekend. But I hadn't decided anything. I hadn't made up my mind. I still could've stayed.

I didn't know why I was so afraid of admitting to myself that I wanted to go, but I was. I felt greedy, but wasn't I allowed to want the best and the most for myself?

I was trapped in this endless cycle of denial and desperate self-validation. I felt like I was on the teacup ride at an amusement park for hours. My stomach flipped and turned and I felt bile rise up in my throat more than a few times. I lied in bed and cried and cried and cried.

August even asked me if I was okay. Normally she ignored it when I got too upset. She wasn't good at handling it, she always said.

"I'm okay."

"Is everything good with your girl?"

A wave of guilt nearly knocked me to my knees. "Everything's great with Sophia."

"Zoe hasn't bothered you, has she?"

"No, I haven't heard from her."

"I'm not gonna keep digging, babe. You can tell me what's up if you want. I can't and won't keep fishing." August rolled onto her stomach.

Did I want to tell her? Would telling another person make it easier or more real? Would August tell me anything I hadn't already thought of? Liliana was right when she said I needed to get out of my own head. Problem was, I didn't have another head to get into. And when people offered me a peek into theirs, I shut them down. I twisted my way out like a trapped animal. I didn't want to hear what they thought because what they thought didn't match up with what I felt. Torn.

My roommate raised an eyebrow at me expectantly. I sighed. "I might transfer schools."

"And you're… crying about it?"

"The other school is in Colorado."

August shrugged. "Haven't you always wanted to go out west after school anyway?" she asked. "What's the problem?"

"I don't want to leave Sophia."

She half rolled her eyes, but caught herself. "Right. Your girl. That sucks, dude," she said with the most empathy I'd ever seen her muster up. I loved my roommate, I really did, but she wasn't the most… feelings-y girl I'd ever met. "But you wanna go, right?"

I nodded, feeling ashamed.

"There are girls in Colorado too, dude," August told me. "She won't do long distance?"

"I haven't told her…"

She sighed heavily. "Christ, Annabella, then stop crying about it until you do. You don't even know what she's going to say. You didn't even say you're definitely leaving. Stop worrying about it." She sounded exhausted and I didn't blame her. I was exhausted. This topic was exhausted. I didn't know why I kept asking people for advice when all I wanted to do was shut them up every time. *No, you don't understand.*

No answer anyone could give me would make me feel better, because what I wanted was impossible.

"I can't just turn my feelings off like you can, August." She snorted. "I feel greedy."

"Anna, babe, you've only been with this girl for like a week." August shook her head. "It doesn't make sense to be so torn up over it. Go to Colorado if that's what you want. That's what you wanted before her, right?"

I nodded halfheartedly.

"Then don't let her change that. Things could still work. And if they don't, there are girls in Colorado."

I took Sophia out to dinner that night with the full intention of talking to her about Colorado. It was all I could think about in the hours leading up to our date. But, of course, once I saw her, the knots in my stomach and chest and throat and head melted away. I almost completely forgot about it.

I was so selfish. I didn't want to talk about it yet. I wanted more time with her. I wanted more good days. I wanted her. I wanted her. I wanted her. Why was I ruining this again? Why couldn't I ever be content with one good thing? Why did I feel like I was being torn in half?

We went to the movie theater down the street from campus to see some crappy horror movie Emma had told her about. Neither of us were horror fans, but the theater was so small that the only thing they were showing besides that was a children's movie. The colors were so plastic and bright that just the trailer gave me a migraine. So horror movie it was.

The theater was empty at eight pm on a Tuesday night, so Sophia and I got prime seats in the exact center of the theater. She put her arm on the rest between us and I rested my head on her shoulder, even though it hurt my neck to do so. The arm rest dug into my ribs but it was a small price to pay to be close to her.

When the lights dimmed, she let her head rest on top of mine. My heart leapt up and hit the top of my head before sinking down to where it belonged. Touching her still drove me wild. There were fireworks underneath my skin. I took her hand and lifted it to my lips, kissing each knuckle. I could feel her pulse quicken and I couldn't not smile.

The trailers rolled and I pretended to watch them. All I could think about was that stupid thread that Liliana told me about. How could I acknowledge the thread, feel its shortness, and still want to go to school two thousand miles away from her? It was enough to be inches away from Sophia. Even now, in the dark movie theater with my head on her shoulder and her head on mine, I didn't feel close enough to her.

Was it possible for every cell in my body to split down the center? There was the Annabella who wanted to go and the Annabella who wanted to stay. I couldn't keep them both happy. I couldn't listen to them both. It seemed foolish to even try.

Sophia lifted her head off of mine just long enough for her to kiss my hair. I wondered if she could hear my thoughts. If she knew that I wanted to go. If she knew that I knew I could love her from two thousand miles away. If she could love me, too.

I knew I was going to Colorado.

I knew I couldn't tell her yet.

We lasted about twenty minutes into the actual film before giving up. We made out under the cover of darkness like two fourteen year olds on their first chaperone-less date. Her tongue slid into my mouth and I never felt so much animosity towards an arm rest in my entire life. This little plastic barrier keeping me from her. Sophia tangled one hand in my hair and I considered breaking it off. I was pretty sure I could, anyway. My hand wandered up her thigh and up across her stomach to her breast. I felt her smile against my lips.

I was gonna lose it.

"Come on," I whispered in her ear, taking her hand. In a fit of giggles, I led her out of the theater and into the bathroom. We holed up in the handicap stall, Sophia pressed up against the door. Neither one of us could stop laughing.

My hands found their way to her waist, peeling up the thin layer of her t-shirt and exposing her smooth, brown skin. Underneath her shirt, one hand made its way back to her breast. I was still amazed at how warm her skin was. She was on fire. I was on fire. The whole damn theater was on fire. My heart was racing. Sophia's hand slid into my back pocket. Her teeth scraped against my lip. I felt like I was going to burst. I felt her fumbling with the button on my jeans. It popped out and I pushed her harder against the door, unintentionally hindering her efforts. My fingers found the button on *her* jeans. I unzipped them slowly, tantalizingly, and my fingers brushed the lace fringe of her underwear. The door creaked.

"Uh… is everything okay in there?" A confused, older woman's voice said from somewhere in the bathroom. I stopped kissing Sophia, whose eyes went wide with surprise. She started to laugh and I covered her mouth with my hand, barely containing my own laugher.

"*Shh*. Everything's fine! I'll be out in a second!" I called to the woman, biting my lip and smiling too hard. I took my hand off of Sophia's mouth. She was smiling so hard that it crinkled her nose. I wanted to kiss her again.

"Are you sure everything's okay, dear?" I heard footsteps. They stopped right outside the stall. "Is it… are you alone in there?"

Sophia snorted.

"Bless you," I said. "No I'm, uh, no. My friend needed me to look at… a tick. She has a tick. On her back." Sophia snorted again. "Bless you," I said, putting my hand back on her mouth. "And a cold." She pinched my butt. "And impulse control issues," I whispered, smirking.

"Oh, alright then…"

"Can you behave?" I whispered. Sophia nodded, brown eyes sincere and pleading. I took my hand off of her mouth and she kissed me. I snorted, pulling back and stepping away from her. She opened the stall door and we walked out.

The elderly woman smiled at us, then frowned at Sophia's waist. "Your pants are unbuttoned, dear."

We lost it. Sophia grabbed my hand and we bolted from the bathroom, nearly collapsing in a fit of giggles when we got back into the theater. She sat down and pulled me on top of her, kissing my lips and jaw and neck. A thousand tiny, fluttering kisses to match the fluttering in my chest.

I almost told her that I loved her then, that I was fairly certain I'd loved her since I met her, but I held my tongue and laughed instead.

"I love how you laugh when I kiss you," Sophia said into my neck. Her breath was hot and sweet. My entire body felt like it was buzzing.

I kissed her forehead, the bridge of her nose, and finally her lips. "I love how you kiss me," I said, mouth just millimeters from hers. She closed the space between our lips. I was flying.

"That's good," she said. "Because I love kissing you."

"I know," I told her. And she laughed.

twenty two
sophia jane kalvak
April 10

Annabella insisted on eating dinner at the dining commons just the two of us. We passed August, sitting by herself, and Emma, sitting with Allison and Elise, and took up a small table in the back corner of the second floor. I didn't know why she wanted to sit away from our friends, but I didn't question it. Like always, I was just happy to be with her.

Something was clearly up, though. She didn't laugh as fully at my jokes as she usually did. She didn't hold up her end of the conversation. She didn't even eat much. She just moved the food around on her plate, staring at it, while I blabbered on about my day and my classes. I kept waiting for her to tell me on her own, but she wouldn't. The empty spaces I left in the conversation remained empty. She didn't interject. She didn't bring it up.

I was starting to worry.

"Okay, what's wrong?"

"What do you mean what's wrong?"

I sighed. "What's going on with you? Clearly something's up." I took her hand. "Talk to me. What's going on, baby?" I asked, squeezing her fingers. She looked like she might throw up.

Annabella took a deep breath, then looked up at me. "I applied to this other college right before I broke up with Zoe. I was freaked out, you know. I wanted to get out of here. I was afraid," she told me. "I forgot about it for a while. And I didn't think I'd get in anyway. It's my dream school. I didn't get into it the first time around."

I wasn't following her. Why would she be upset about applying to another school over a month ago? Was it about Zoe? Where was she going with this? I didn't understand. I felt stupid.

"Anyway, I got an email from them… a while ago." Annabella winced. How long ago was 'a while ago'? "I got in."

So she got into another school. It took a second for it to register with me what that meant. "Are you… transferring?" I felt something in my chest deflate. Annabella nodded, eyes watery. The deflated balloon in my chest seemed to freeze. Why would she leave? "What school?" I asked hesitantly.

"University of Colorado."

"*Colorado?*" The balloon shattered. Everything in me shattered. I wouldn't have been surprised if every glass object in the entire dining hall shattered. The windows, the plates, the bowls, the cups, the mugs. A sea of glass. I could feel the shards in my skin.

Annabella nodded again. "I sent my deposit and my acceptance this morning. I'm so sorry, Sophia. This is my dream school. They have one of the best psych programs out there. I'm sorry. I couldn't say no." She was crying. My eyes were strangely dry.

"When did you find out?"

"Does it matter?"

"How long have you been keeping this from me? How long have you been lying to me?"

"I'm not lying to you, Sophia. I haven't lied to you." Her voice was small. I started to feel bad for her before I realized that *I* was small. Not my voice. Me. I was small. I was insignificant. The truth of it shook me.

I didn't stop, though. I wasn't sure that I could. "Not telling the truth is lying, Annabella. When did you get the email?"

She ducked her head. "The 31st."

My throat tied itself in a knot. "Great, so our entire relationship is bullshit, then? You've been lying to me the entire time? Did you—did you know when you asked me to be your girlfriend? You know what, I don't want to know. It doesn't matter." She shook her head anyway. "What the hell, Annabella? What the hell was the point of any of this then?"

"What?"

"You're breaking up with me, right? That's what you're doing? What was this, then, some…

trial period? To see if I was good enough to stay for?" Now I was crying. "I thought you cared about me. I thought... I don't know what I thought. I don't know why I thought anything. I barely know you. I don't know what I was thinking. I wasn't thinking." I wiped my eyes. Annabella was still crying. People were staring. "You're breaking up with me, right? Say it."

"I'm not breaking up with you, Sophia."

"You're moving to Colorado in the fall, Annabella."

"Are you breaking up with *me*?"

My muscles froze all at once. I stared at her. "No, I'm not. I'm not doing anything. You're the one doing this. I don't know why you didn't just break up with me on the spot. Why didn't you just tell me? I would have understood. It would've been better than lying to me for two weeks. You could've hit the reset button. We could've been friends instead of exes."

"I'm not breaking up with you, Sophia. I want this to work. I want to make this work. I do care about you. That's why I didn't tell you until now. Because I hadn't decided. I didn't want... this wasn't easy for me. I care about you so much," Annabella said, wiping her eyes. "Sit down, please." I hadn't realized I was standing. I complied. She reached for my hand but I pulled it onto my lap. "I don't want to lose you, but I can't miss out on this opportunity," she explained. "I will see you every day of every vacation if that's what you want. I will call you every single day. I'll do anything, okay? Just. Don't leave me."

"You're the one leaving me, Annabella."
Her name didn't taste quite the same. I started to cry
again. "Jesus Christ, I feel so stupid. This shouldn't
hurt as bad as it does. I barely know you."

"Stop saying that. You do know me. And I
know you. And we can make things work."
Annabella frowned. "I know we haven't been
together that long. I know we haven't known each
other that long. But we do know each other, Sophia.
And I can't and won't speak for you, but I care
about you deeply. You mean a lot to me. I've
never... I've never felt so much for someone so
quickly. I don't want to throw that away," she said.
"I meant what I said about the threads."

"You said our thread was short. You said
being apart felt straining. How can you mean that
and want to move, what, three thousand miles
away?"

"Two," she corrected me, then shook her
head. "Maybe I was wrong about that. Maybe our
thread is longer than that. Maybe it can stretch from
Colorado to New Hampshire and not break."

I shook my head. It didn't make any sense.

"Can we at least try, Sophia?" Annabella's
voice sounded broken. "Please? Can we try?"

"I need some time to think."

"Okay... I understand." She sounded hurt.
Some gross, bitter part of me was almost happy
with that. But it was the minority. The rest of me
wanted to reach out and wrap my arms around her
and kiss her and never let go. All of me wanted to
lay in bed in the dark and cry.

"I'll... I'll talk to you later, I guess." I stood. "I don't... I need to go home."

I wanted her to stop me when I walked away, but she didn't. She just sat there. It didn't occur to me until much later that that was what she expected me to do. Sit there. Let her leave.

Maybe I should have.

I felt foolish for crying. Every tear I shed came with a disclaimer of irrationality. I wasn't in love with Annabella, I couldn't be. I had only dated her for less than two weeks, only known her for a month. Everything about this was too quick. Our friendship. Our relationship. The end of it. It was like someone hit the fast forward button on the TV remote, not realizing that this was Real Life and not some rom com they could skip past.

It was irrational. I wasn't in love with her. But my heart was broken. Because I knew I could have been. So easily.

She hadn't broken up with me, though. She wanted to make things work between us. But she wanted them to work from two thousand miles away. One thousand, nine hundred and twelve-point-two miles, actually. I Googled it.

It was a four hour flight from Boston, a twenty nine hour drive, a six hundred and fourteen hour walk.

Could it work from that distance? Could she love me from Colorado? Could I love her? Was it even worth trying? I cared about her. I wanted her. I liked her. But I didn't want to get my heart broken for real. Even this was painful enough.

The door opened and Emma came in. I pulled the blankets over my head. She sat down beside me. "What happened, Sophia?"

"Annabella is transferring to the University of Colorado next semester," I said. It was too hot under the blanket already, but I didn't want to come out. I didn't want Emma to see me. I felt stupid. I felt so stupid.

Emma rested her hand on my hip. "Did she break up with you?"

"No."

"Well that's good, right?"

"Good would be her not leaving."

Emma sighed. "I know, Soph, but that's not what's happening. What are you going to do?"

"I don't know." I didn't know anything and it was making me feel sick. I wanted anything. Some semblance of certainty. Some idea of what the best choice would have been. I couldn't figure it out on my own. I wanted to ask everyone I had ever known. I wanted to see a psychic. I wanted someone to make my decision for me because I was too scared. I didn't want to make the wrong choice and own up to it when I was wrong. I wanted someone to point fingers at. To blame.

I was being a child about this. But I knew that. And knowing had to count for something, right?

I knew in the end I would make my own decision, regardless of the temper tantrum I was throwing in the meantime.

She was quiet for a minute. "I think you should stay with her."

I knew Emma would think that. I knew she was right, too. Christ, I knew that that was what I was going to do. I knew I wouldn't leave her. Why was I even throwing this fit? Why was I even trying to talk myself out of it? "What if I get hurt?"

"What if you don't?" Emma asked. "You're already hurting, there's no point in trying to avoid more hurt. That's... that's just life. Everyone gets hurt. It happens. She'll hurt you and you'll hurt her. I'm sorry, but it's inevitable." She wasn't making me feel any better. "But I've never seen you happier than you are when you're around her. I think it would be dumb of you to throw that away because of distance. I think it would be dumb of you to not at least give it a try."

"Maybe..." She was right, she was right, she was right. My mind was made up. It was never un-made. I was looking for validation. I wanted her to tell me I was right. I wanted her to think that I was thinking through this and that my decision hadn't been made before I even left the table.

I felt so melodramatic. But I needed this, somehow.

"What's the worst that could happen?"

"I could fall in love with her. I could fall in love with her in the meantime, before she leaves. And it could hurt even worse when she does. It's not like she's leaving right now or tomorrow or even next week. She isn't leaving for four months. Which sounds good on paper but in reality that's just more time for me to fall for her, Emma. That's more time for me to love her. More things to miss when she leaves." I pulled the blanket off of my head and sat up. "I'm scared."

It felt so good to say it. So I said it again.

Emma frowned. "I know you are. But that's why I think you need to try. You wouldn't be scared if she didn't mean a lot to you already. You wouldn't be scared if this wasn't something worth doing."

What she was saying made sense, but I wasn't very good at doing things I was afraid of. Although, I was getting better at it. Annabella was helping me get better at it. At being less afraid.

"So you think I should stay with her?"

"I know you should. And so do you," Emma said firmly. "It's only eight months out of the year. For two more years. That's sixteen months apart. Which sounds like a lot but in the grand scheme of things, is it really? Do you think she's worth it?"

I nodded hesitantly.

"Then how could you not give it a try?" Emma asked. "And besides, a lot can happen in four months. You guys could break up before she leaves, anyway. Which I don't think will happen, but you could. This could be a complete nonissue. But if you break up with her now you'll never know," she told me. "It'll always feel unfinished. You'll never be able to actually... get over her. You know? You have to just let things play out. See where they go."

"I guess..."

"Now isn't the time to break up with her. You're just getting started. Trust me," Emma sighed. "You don't want that unfinished feeling.

You don't want the 'what if's'. They absolutely suck. You want to try."

I groaned, but I wasn't really upset anymore. It was more for theatrics than anything else. "I hate when you're right."

"No you don't." Emma laughed.

I rolled onto my back, staring up at the ceiling. "Should I call her?"

"Do you want to call her?"

I sighed, closing my eyes. "Yes. No. I don't know." A bitter, sad part of me wanted her to stew in it for a little while. I didn't want to tell her I was staying with her yet. I wanted her to worry about losing me. But I knew that was unfair and mean.

"You're going to stay with her?"

"Yes."

"Then you should call her. Don't keep her waiting on an answer. That's not fair," Emma said, as if she read my mind.

"None of this is fair." I pulled my pillow over my face. I wanted to scream into it, but I refrained. I felt like crawling under my bed and crying, even though I wasn't as sad as I was before. I was exhausted. I wanted to cry it out.

"Call her."

"Yes, mom."

twenty three

annabella morgan avery
April 11

Seeing Sophia the next day felt like walking on eggshells. She didn't act any differently towards me—she was a bigger woman than I was—but I was so afraid that she would. That anything I said or did would make her snap. I was projecting, I knew it, but I couldn't bring myself to walk on flat feet.

I was just so lucky she was staying with me. That she cared about me enough to want to make things work. So when I asked if she wanted to talk about it and she said no, I didn't push her. Maybe it was wrong of me. Maybe I should have talked to her about it more instead of pretending it didn't exist. But I didn't want her to change her mind. I didn't want to talk her out of wanting me.

I didn't want to ruin my chance before it even started. I didn't want to lose her before I even left. I didn't want to lose her sunlight, her warmth, *her*.

August invited us to the dining commons with her and her flavor of the week. I couldn't remember the poor girl's name, but I hastily accepted the invitation anyway. My roommate never cared to even tell me the names of the girls she was 'seeing', let alone invite me to lunch with them. Maybe this girl was different. I hoped so, anyway. It would be good for August, I thought. She needed some sort of normal consistency. She needed some sort of… emotion. Something.

Sophia and I arrived before them, staking claim to a smaller, round table on the second floor. Our meals sat untouched on our plates as we sipped water, waiting for them to arrive. I was nervous, but had no real reason to be. I jiggled my leg underneath the table until Sophia put her hand on my knee. Her touch settled most, if not all, of my nerves. I tentatively set my foot down. Nothing seemed to shatter. A knot in my back loosened and I relaxed my shoulders.

"Are you okay?" Sophia asked.

I nodded. "Don't worry about it." She smiled at me, but I knew she would worry regardless.

They were over twenty minutes late. "Maybe she changed her mind," I said finally. "Maybe they're not coming." Sophia shrugged.

"Maybe who's not coming? I'm right on time, babe." August's voice came from behind me. "You guys are just early." She sat down across from me with a girl I'd never seen before. She was tall—taller than Sophia—with wide hips and thick, dark lips. Her black, dreaded hair brushed her waist. "This is Emily. Emily, this is my roommate, Anna, and her girlfriend, Sophia." Emily smiled and lifted her hand in a halfhearted attempt at a wave, but didn't say anything. Sophia and I exchanged innocuous glances.

We suffered through the obligatory twenty-ish minutes of small talk with clenched jaws. My nerves were returning slowly, but I held Sophia's hand under the table to keep the worst of them at bay. I was never uncomfortable with meeting new people before; I didn't know why I was reacting this way today. Maybe it was just the new person in combination with the rest of the stress I was dealing with lately. Maybe I was just tired.

August didn't treat Emily like she was anything special. Most of her comments were directed towards either Sophia or myself. Emily mainly stayed silent, interjecting only with quick, four-to-five word quips. I wondered if she was shy or if we just weren't giving her enough space to talk. I tried to direct questions towards the poor girl, but August either answered for her or changed the subject.

I shot my roommate a harsh glance, to which she only stared innocently back. I wasn't sure if she knew what she was doing or not, but it was uncomfortable for everyone else involved. "August, I have to pee, can you come with me?"

"Your girl is right there, Anna."

"Yeah, I know, come with me."

I took her into the alcove by the bathroom, stopping before the door. "Why are you being so rude to Emily?"

August snorted. "I'm not being rude. What are you talking about?"

"You won't let the poor girl talk."

"She's not that interesting. I'm doing you a favor."

I threw my arms up in the air. "Then why are you with her? Why did you want me to meet her?" I asked. August folded her arms across her chest. "You're ridiculous, August. Be nicer to her or don't pretend you're doing anything but hooking up. It's fine if you don't like her, no one's forcing you to, but it's idiotic to pretend it's more than sex if it's not. Since when do you do that, anyway?"

August didn't say anything.

"Are you going to tell me what's going on?"

"No."

I wanted to press her further, to make her talk about this with me, but I knew it wouldn't do any good. August didn't do the feelings thing well. Which is why none of this made sense. Why was she making me meet this girl if she didn't like her? If she was, quote, not that interesting? It didn't make any sense. But I was tired of trying to make sense of my roommate's behaviors regarding women. "Fine, don't tell me. You've got some real issues, dude, and I know it's none of my business but maybe you should consider working those out before you drag some poor girl into it."

"You're right," August said. "It *is* none of your business."

I rolled my eyes and pushed past her, heading back to the table. "It was really nice meeting you, Emily, but Sophia and I have to go," I said, picking up my plates. Sophia looked up at me, confused, but stood as well. "See you around," I said with a forced smile.

"Nice meeting you," Sophia said, still looking at me.

Emily frowned. "Oh, uh. It was nice meeting you guys, too. Where is August?" She leaned to the side to look past me. I turned around to see that she wasn't there.

"Um, bathroom still, I think." I grimaced. If August had left this poor girl here I was going to *kill* her. "Anyway… um. Have a good one."

"You too…"

I didn't think I had ever walked down a flight of stairs that quickly in my life. "What was that about?" Sophia asked, trailing after me. "What was August's deal?"

I shook my head. "I have no idea. It's not my problem."

"No, it's not, but—"

"I don't really want to talk about this, Soph. I'm annoyed. I just want to go home. Do you want to come with me?" I asked, placing my dishes on the conveyer belt to be taken into the washroom. She nodded, setting her dishes down too. I took her hand and forced a smile.

My room was freezing. August had left the window open when she left, and it was one of those bitter April days that seemed to be convinced it was a February night. The first thing I did when I got in the room was close the window, closely followed by stripping off my jeans and burying myself under my blankets. Sophia peeled off her jeans and crawled under them with me. Her warmth did more to warm me than the fabric covering me ever could.

Underneath the covers, we talked about nothing significant. The cold. The children we saw earlier. The test I had coming up next week. My upcoming birthday. The sweater I was wearing. Nothing of consequence, nothing important, nothing riveting. And yet I didn't want to stop talking. I wanted this moment, this mundane bit of meaningless small talk. And a hundred thousand more.

I touched my frozen toes to her leg and she laughed, pulling away. "Stop, you're so cold!"

"Yeah? Warm me up, then," I teased, kissing her on the nose. When I pulled away from her, her face moved with me. As if pulled by a magnet.

Sophia raised one eyebrow, then pulled me close to her and kissed me. The kisses were soft and fluttering at first but grew heavier and hungrier. I felt her hands on me, burning me, and I realized I had been starving. Her fingers danced along the edge of my underwear, teasing, and I couldn't help but smile and pull her closer to me. She could crack my ribcage open and crawl inside and she wouldn't have been close enough.

Slowly, still kissing, we sat up and I moved on top of her. She was laughing as she pulled off my sweater. Laughing as I pulled off hers. She kissed me again, her hand traveling up my back and unhooking my bra. I shrugged out of it and tossed it on the floor with the rest of her clothes, then took hers off and tossed it, too. I was amazed at how easy it was. How easy all of this felt.

Nothing on earth felt as good as her skin on mine. Her fingers traced invisible patterns on my body as my hungry hands and mouth pulled her closer and closer to me. Sophia laid down underneath me and I kissed her neck, her collarbone, the space between her breasts, her naval, the inside of each thigh. I could feel her pulse pounding everywhere my fingers brushed, everywhere my lips touched, keeping stride with mine.

Sophia was half asleep in my arms. I could feel her nodding off every few seconds, only to jerk herself awake. I kissed her forehead after one of these snaps. "Just go to sleep, baby," I told her, kissing her again. "I'll wake you up in an hour or two. I've got to go to bed pretty early tonight anyway. I'll just wake you when I want to sleep, okay?"

"Why do you need to go to bed early? And I'm not tired," she told me, but her heavy eyelids were already sliding shut again.

I hesitated. "I have to be up early for my flight." I'd forgotten to tell her about the campus tour, hadn't I? I cursed myself internally. I didn't want the mention of Colorado to ruin what had been shaping up to be a pretty excellent day. I brushed my thumb against the bare skin of her hip. "For the tour."

"What tour?" Sophia's eyes were still closed. She was still floating somewhere between sleep and wake.

I sighed. "Of the University of Colorado. Didn't I tell you? I scheduled a tour. I'm flying out tomorrow," I said, feeling a pit open up in my stomach. "I thought I told you."

She didn't open her eyes, but they were squeezed tight now. Not the eyes of someone who was just tired. She didn't want to open them. "You're leaving tomorrow?"

"Just for the day, baby," I said. "I'll be back late tomorrow night. I'm not even spending the night there." My words sounded more like a promise than a statement. *I'm not leaving you yet. I'll be back. I won't be gone for long.* I was worried if I spoke anymore they would start to sound more like an apology than a promise.

Sophia nestled her head closer to my chest, pressing her lips to me. "Will you wake me up when you get home? Will you come to my room?" she asked. She sounded sad but resolved to it. Comfortable in it, almost. I felt guilty for the way her question washed away the knots in me. For the way I was relieved that she still wanted me tomorrow. That she wanted me as soon as I got back.

"Of course I will, if that's what you want. It'll be pretty late, though," I said. I knew she would still want me to wake her, but I wanted to hear her say it again. I wasn't trying to convince her, I was trying to convince me.

Her mouth was still pressed to the skin below my collarbone. I could feel her lips move as she spoke. The heat from her breath spread outward from the place she touched me, slowly spilling over me. "That's what I want."

"Then I'll wake you up as soon as I get back," I said.

"Do you promise?"

"I promise."

"Thank you, Annabella." She turned her face to me, lifting one eyelid just enough to see me. I kissed her. She smiled, closed her eye, and then nestled her head back against my chest.

My space heater girlfriend fell asleep almost instantly. I could feel the shift in her breathing, slower and deeper now. Her heat got caught under the blanket, warming every inch of me.

I couldn't help but think about how cold Colorado would be.

twenty four

sophia jane kalvak
April 12

Knowing Annabella wasn't even in the state by the time that I woke up the next morning made me feel inexplicably wintery and cold. When I looked out the window, I was genuinely surprised to see newly sprouted green instead of endless blankets of white. I laid back down and pulled my blankets up to my nose, feeling foolish. She would only be gone for the day. There was no reason for me to be sad.

Although, the reason she was gone for the day was a side effect of her soon leaving for months. For 2/3 of the year.

But I didn't want to think about that.

Emma and I had plans to spend the day together. Aside from quick conversations between class and before bed, I felt like I never saw her anymore. We never hung out one on one. I was always with Annabella or she was always with Jarred. Despite my imaginary chill, it was a beautiful day out, and we decided to head downtown to walk around and window shop. I had to get Annabella's birthday present soon, and I had absolutely no idea where to start.

It seemed as though half the campus and a third of the surrounding town had the same idea that we did. The usually mellow main street was bustling that afternoon. Everyone was pushing carriages of moody giggling crying sneezing children or walking sniffing grumbling tail-wagging dogs.

We linked arms as we walked down the sidewalk, ruminating on ideas for Annabella's birthday present. There were plenty of things my girlfriend liked, sure, but she never really seemed to *want* anything. Anything she wanted she went out and bought for herself. She wasn't the type to pine after something or even really mention it to anyone else. She just got it, because the things she genuinely wanted or needed were so few and far between.

I couldn't exactly get my girlfriend something as impersonal as a gift card, though. So Emma and I continued bouncing ideas off of each other. She didn't know her well enough to have any solid suggestions or feedback, but it was nice to have a sounding board. It was nice to talk to my best friend about something that wasn't sad. It had been a while since we'd done that.

"How are you two, anyway?" Emma asked, taking an extra-large stride to avoid stepping on a crack between two segments of sidewalk. "Are you getting along?"

I nodded. "Yeah, we're good. I was worried things would be awkward after her telling me about Colorado. I mean, it was for a little bit after I told her I didn't want to break up. But it went back to normal pretty fast." I kicked a crushed tin can to the side, closer to a trash can. A dog watched it skid across the sidewalk with near-desperate eyes. She wandered up to me as I walked by, tail wagging. I wanted to pet her, but her owner tugged on her leash and led her away. I tried not to be too disappointed.

"And normal is good?"

I snapped back into the conversation. "Better than good," I told her. "I'm really happy with her. I like how she makes me feel."

Emma smiled. "Good. I'm glad you're happy, Sophia. You deserve it." Her words warmed something in my core. It was nice to get some form of approval of my relationship.

"Thanks," I said. "Hey. Guess what happened yesterday."

Emma glanced at me, eyebrow raised. "What happened yesterday?" she asked, smirking slightly.

"Annabella and I had sex," I told her, trying not to smile like an idiot.

Emma shoved me playfully, laughing. "You did *not!*" she said. "It's about damn time," she joked. "So, how was it? Gimme all the details."

I laughed. "It was good…"

"*Good?*"

"It was real good," I told her. "I don't know. It wasn't like I expected it to be."

"In a good way or a bad way?"

"A good way, definitely. It was better than I expected. Not even just the sex, just the. I don't know. Being with her. Being close to her like that." I could feel my face getting hot. "It was good."

Emma laughed again. "Good, I'm happy for you. My little baby, all grown up and fucking girls," she said, pretending to wipe a tear away from her eye. "So, Sophia, how exactly *do* lesbians have sex?"

I shoved her. "Cut it out, don't ask me that." I snorted. "You know how lesbians have sex, Emma." I rolled my eyes. "It's like all the parts of straight sex that actually feel good for you," I teased. "But better, I'd assume, because girls know what feels good."

Emma snorted. "Fair enough. Sex with Jarred *was*, objectively, terrible," she told me. "That's one thing I for sure won't miss about him."

"Won't miss?"

My roommate looked down at the ground. "Yeah, Jarred and I broke up. I broke up with him, I mean. Last night."

"Oh," I said. They broke up all the time. It wasn't anything to write home about. It wasn't anything worth acknowledging. They'd be back together next week and she'd be miserable again. I'd lost count of the amount of times they'd broken up since the first time they got together. It was exhausting to even try to keep up with it all.

"For real this time," Emma said. "I'm serious. I'm not getting back with him. He's bad for me. I don't feel good when I'm with him. I don't have fun with him." She sighed heavily. "I want someone I can have fun with. Someone nice. Someone genuine," she said. "I want what you and Annabella have, to be honest."

"Well I'll see if we can't find you a nice girlfriend," I teased.

Emma grinned. "Oh, would you please?"

My mom called me again that night. I was sitting in bed, still naked and wrapped in a towel almost two and a half hours after my shower. My half-damp hair was piled on the top of my head in the sorriest excuse for a bun. I turned to the phone so quickly that it almost fell out. One particularly wet tendril fell and slapped me in the face. I wiped it away and picked up my phone. Her name stared up at me on the screen and I winced.

My thumb hovered over the green button. Did I want to talk to her? Was she worth talking to? The phone vibrated in my hand and I waved my thumb around, as if movement would lead me to a decision. *This is the second time she's called, though...* I thought, recalling the other night when I had been too busy comforting Annabella to even think about talking to my mom.

I hit the button and put the phone to my ear. I did not say anything. I wondered how she'd like the silent treatment.

"Sophia?"

I took a deep breath and let it out all at once, but I didn't give her the satisfaction of a verbal response. She didn't deserve it. Maybe it was childish, but she was going to have to earn me back. She didn't deserve me. Not after the way she had treated me.

"Sophia, are you there?" She sounded tired and sad. Some angry, bitter part of me was glad about that. It wanted her to be sad. She hurt me. I was sad, too. It only seemed fair for her to be sad. "I guess I deserve this," she said, sighing. *You do.* "I'm sorry, baby. I'm sorry." Was she crying? It sounded like it. There was a broken sounding lift to her voice when she said 'sorry' for the second time. A jump in octave that didn't seem planned.

I thought that maybe I should answer her now, but I wasn't sure that I could. My tongue seemed to be tied up. Or shriveling away. Or stuck to the roof of my mouth. Regardless, it was otherwise occupied in a way that would inhibit speaking. I grunted noncommittally, but the sound was so soft I wasn't sure she could hear it. I wasn't sure I wanted her to.

"Please talk to me."

"Like you talked to me?"

"Baby…"

"Don't call me that. Don't—just don't, okay? You hurt me. You're my *mother*. You are supposed to love me. You are supposed to take care of me. You are supposed to support me and keep me safe and care about me no matter what. You're supposed to want me to be happy," I said, my face burning. "But you couldn't. Why?"

"I was wrong..."

"I know you were wrong! You're always wrong. You're bitter and bigoted and callous and *wrong*. Congratulations, you figured it out. You learned right from wrong. It only took you what, fifty years?" I stopped myself. I didn't want to yell at her anymore. I didn't want to fight with her anymore. It was taking too much out of me. It wasn't worth it.

"I said I'm sorry..."

"If I said I was the Queen of France, would it mean anything to you? Would it make it true?"

"Sophia," she said, and I could actually hear her heart break. "Please give me another chance."

"I gave you chances when I called you, mom. You didn't pick up. You didn't want your chances."

"Can't you see it from my side, Sophia? Everything I've been taught to believe said that what you are doing is wrong. That you, my *baby*, are going to hell. Can't you see how I would be scared and angry?"

"Do you think I was scared, Mom? Do you think I was scared when you left me *on the side of the road alone?*" I asked, incredulous. My voice was soft now. I couldn't muster up the hardness. I couldn't find my anger. "I was terrified, Mom. I trusted you. I wanted to, anyway. I wanted to be able to trust that my mom could still love me."

"I do still love you."

"You haven't been acting like it."

"I don't know what else to tell you, Sophia. I'm sorry. I don't understand why you're doing this. I don't understand why you're…"

"A lesbian?" I could hear her flinch.

"I don't understand it, but I love you. Give me a chance, please?" she asked. "Let me try to understand. Let me start over." I sighed. "I can't promise I'll get it all right this time, but I'll try. Please just let me try, baby."

"I don't know."

"Can I meet her?" She sounded both hopeful and sick at the same time. I wasn't sure which hurt me more.

"Who?" I asked. I didn't want her anywhere near Annabella. I didn't want her to embarrass me. I didn't want her to hurt anyone else. But I wanted to hear her say it.

There was a long pause. "Your girlfriend."

I was almost impressed, despite myself. "I don't think that's a good idea."

"Please? I can drive up next weekend. I can meet her and her parents. I'll behave, Sophia. Please. I want to be a part of your life."

I imagined my mom in a room with Calliope and Eleanor and almost laughed. It would be a disaster, sure, but it would be a funny one. If I managed to live through it to tell the tale. "I'll ask her. Don't get your hopes up. She's not too happy with you, either." Emma walked back into the room. "I have to go. I don't want to talk anymore."

"I love you, Sophia."

"I'll let you know."

I was awoken from a very shallow sleep by a quiet knock on my door. I crawled to the edge of my bed and reached for the doorknob, pulling it open just enough for whoever was on the other side to come in.

"Hey." It was, of course, Annabella. "Did I wake you?" She closed the door behind her and the thin ray of light from the hallway vanished. I could barely see her in the reddish glow from the lights outside.

"No," I said. It was a half-truth. "Come to bed." I reached for her in the dimness, my fingers curling around hers and leading her around the bedframe. I heard her unzip her jeans and step out of them. A moment later, there was a whisper of a thud as her sweatshirt fell to the floor.

She crawled into bed with me, pulling the covers over both of our heads. I could barely make out her face in the darkness after my eyes adjusted.

"How was your tour?" I asked, but I didn't want to hear about it. It felt like asking how the woman she was leaving me for looked. But I was trying not to be bitter.

"It was good," she told me. "But I don't want to talk about it. I missed you." She scooched herself closer to me, pressing her frozen toes to my legs. Her icy fingers raised goose bumps under my t-shirt as they traveled along the smooth plane of my skin. "How was your day?" she asked as my fingers burned pathways on the frozen tundra of her thigh.

"It was okay. I talked to my mom."

Her hands stopped. "You did?"

"She apologized. She says she wants to meet you and your moms." Annabella snorted. "That was about my reaction, too."

"Do you think it's a good idea?"

"I think there have been worse ideas."

She laughed again, and then kissed me on the nose. "I'll do whatever you want, baby."

"Whatever I want?" I asked.

Annabella laughed and kissed my lips. I didn't think I would ever get used to the rush of kissing her. The softness of her mouth. The flowers that blossomed wherever she touched me. The way she tasted of lavender and sunsets and honey. I would never get over any of it. I would never get used to any of it. To her.

I felt her lips brush my jaw as she whispered, "Whatever you want."

Neither one of us was cold anymore.

twenty five
annabella morgan avery
April 19

Cora drove Sophia and me back home the next weekend. She was hyperactive; twitchy; anxious. She spent the entire car ride asking Sophia questions about her mother. How religious was she? Had she sounded sincere in her apology? Would she say or do anything to hurt me? Liliana? Our Moms? Why did she apologize so suddenly? Could she have been lying? How are you, Sophia? Are you nervous, too?

Sophia fielded the questions in a monotone voice, not looking up from her hands. I turned around in the front seat (Cora hated when we both sat in the back, it made her feel like a chauffeur). She looked up at me and faked a smile, but it didn't come close to touching her eyes. I took her hand.

"Don't worry. Moms aren't gonna put up with any bigoted bullshit. She says something wrong, she's out." I kissed her fingers.

Sophia sighed. "That's what I'm worried about," she told me in a hushed voice. "I don't think she'll say something purposely malicious. I mean, I hope she won't anyway. But I'm worried she'll say or do something by accident and hurt everyone and not realize it. She's... I don't think she's ever even met a gay person before."

"She birthed one," I joked, but Sophia didn't laugh. "Well neither had you, right?" She shrugged. "You did just fine." I was floundering. I didn't know what to say to make her feel better and it was making me feel all knotted up inside. "There's no use worrying, baby. What happens, happens. I'll tell Moms to go easy on her, okay?" I told her. "No making out in the kitchen. Take the Homosexual Agenda off the fridge. Hide all the rainbows."

Sophia smiled. It was tiny, but it was real. "You're too good for me," she told me. "I don't deserve you."

"Shh, of course you do. You deserve the world."

"This is almost as bad as seeing Moms make out, Anna. Quit it." Cora made gagging noises from the driver's seat. We laughed, and I squeezed Sophia's hand.

"It's gonna be okay," I told her. "Try not to worry about it, baby. Moms aren't gonna let anything happen," I said. "I'm not going to let anything happen."

Sophia squeezed my hand back. "I know. Thank you."

Her mom was late. We sat around the kitchen counter, eating the dip Mom had made with the pita bread Ma bought, and pretending not to watch the clock. Even over the small talk, I could hear it ticking. There was a growing sense of discomfort with every tick.

I wasn't sure why I was so nervous. Wouldn't it probably be *better* if Sophia's mom never showed up at all? Wouldn't we be better off? No crisis could occur if she never came around. The gnawing in my gut didn't care about that, though. I looked over at my girlfriend, the only person not talking, and felt angry. Angry at her mother for doing this. Angry at her for hurting her, getting her hopes up, and then letting her down again. Angry.

It swelled up in my gut and I felt it in my jaw and in my arms. Tension. Aching. My hands balled up into fists and something in my throat wanted to fly out of my mouth but I kept it clamped shut tight.

Tick, tick, tick.

Finally, there was a knock at the door. The woman standing at the door couldn't have been Sophia's mother. She looked nothing like her. She was short, thin, and white. Her hair was a fiery shade of orange. She looked terrified and, well, *weak.* Like a moderately strong gust of wind could blow her away. Like she wouldn't even fight it.

Could a woman like that raise a woman like Sophia?

Sophia opened the door and let her in. Her mother's wide, green eyes jumped from face to face. Then down to Moms' hands, fingers intertwined on top of the counter. Her eyes jolted back up and she offered and uncomfortable smile. She turned to Sophia and whispered something I couldn't hear. My girlfriend rolled her eyes.

"This is my mom, Olivia," she said. "Mom, this is Liliana and Cora." She gestured to my sisters, who waved uncomfortably. "My girlfriend, Annabella." She locked eyes with me for a brief moment. I smiled at her encouragingly. "And their Moms, Calliope and Eleanor." Mom waved, Ma smiled tightly.

Olivia lifted a limp hand in some sort of impression of a wave. "It's nice to meet all of you," she said. Even her voice sounded meek.

"It's lovely to meet you as well, Olivia," Mom said, using her Teacher Voice. I'd been with her when she bumped into ex-students she hated or particularly annoying parents in the grocery store or at the mall enough times to be able to pick it out immediately. "Why don't we move to the living room?" she suggested. Cora took the dip and what remained of the pita bread off of the counter and relocated it to the coffee table.

Mom nudged Ma, prompting her to speak. "Do you want anything to drink?" Was all she was able to come up with.

Olivia shook her head. "No, I'm fine, thank you." Her arms were clasped tightly to her side. She looked so *stiff.* It was almost comical, if we weren't the reasons for her stiffness. If I didn't know it was disgust keeping her muscles locked.

We sat in the living room and Mom tried her best to make small talk with Olivia. She asked what she did for work, what church she went to, as well as a myriad of other mom-like questions that I couldn't make myself follow or care about.

Sophia and I claimed the loveseat on the other side of the living room, as far away from Olivia (on the edge of the arm chair by the doorway) as we could be. I could feel her watching us, so I made a point to constantly be touching my girlfriend. I held her hand, I played with her fingers, I rubbed circles and figure-eights on her thigh, and I played with her hair. It was childish, sure, but I could either be immature or I could be angry. I told myself that I would be touching Sophia anyway, whether her mom was there or not. Which wasn't untrue.

Mom seemed stuck on the topic of religion. Maybe because that was the only thing any of us knew for sure that Olivia was into. She talked to her about the different churches and synagogues and mosques we went to during her religious phase. Olivia looked marginally less uncomfortable while they remained in a realm she was familiar with.

"Well I'm Catholic, of course," she said. "I always have been."

Mom nodded. "Have you always been so convicted? I've tried a multitude of religions. Most Abrahamic but not all. Nothing ever stuck with me."

Olivia frowned slightly but quickly caught herself. "Well, no, I guess not. When I was younger I was agnostic for a while. Around the time I met Sophia's father, Daniel, actually. And up until he got sick. That's when I really found God," she explained.

I wondered how Sophia's life would've differed if her mom hadn't found God in her husband's sickness. If her father had never even gotten sick.

"And you believe... all of it?" Mom asked incredulously. "Every piece of Catholicism? How interesting. It must be comforting to have a religion that fits so well with you."

Olivia looked at Sophia. "Most of it." Sophia turned her head away and her mother's gaze dropped. "It is nice, though. To have found the truth."

Your truth, I wanted to correct her. I could see Mom wanted to say that, too, but we held our respective tongues.

"I've been thinking about trying religion again," Mom said after some silence. "I was brought up Catholic, so even though I don't believe in it anymore, it seems strange to have nothing in place of it," she told Olivia. "But Eleanor and the kids aren't really interested." She turned to Sophia. "Do you go to church, dear?"

"She goes," Olivia answered for her.

Mom was still looking at Sophia. She made a face, but Sophia's mother couldn't see.

"I do when I'm home," Sophia said. "But I don't believe it." She looked from my mother to hers. "The church hasn't always been welcoming. Catholicism hasn't done me a lot of good as of late."

Her mother didn't say anything, but she dropped her gaze immediately.

Sensing that Mom had made a mistake in asking, Ma jumped in. "Girls, why don't you go out and get a head start on setting the table. And check on dinner while you're out there, please."

"All four of us?" Liliana made a face.

"Yes, all four of you," Ma said. "Thank you."

We slid out of the room quietly, leaving a frightened Olivia alone with Moms. Sophia and I exchanged a look and I shrugged. I had no idea what they were doing. I hardly ever did.

She looked worried.

"Don't worry, baby. I'm sure they just want to talk to her. Mom will keep Ma in line. They'll behave."

She frowned. "But why would they send us out of the room?"

I shrugged. "To be honest, I have no idea. But you just have to trust them, I guess. Mom's dealt with this kind of shit from her parents. She'll know what to do, I think."

"Do her parents talk to her now?"

I tried not to make a face as I handed her the good plates from the cupboard. "Not exactly... but practice makes perfect, right? Your mom's here. She's trying. That's more than Mom's parents ever did. I haven't even met them," I told her. "Just. Let them talk for a while. Let her see how normal they are. How in love they are," I said. "I think it'll be easier for her that way. Because right now she's seeing two separate Sophia's, you know? The one she raised and the one who likes girls. If she can see my Moms as normal, maybe she can reconcile the two Sophia's." The words weren't coming out exactly like I wanted them to, but Sophia was nodding as she took the plates to the table.

"They'll be fine," Cora called from the kitchen. "Dinner is almost ready anyway. They won't have long." She shut the oven door.

Liliana, at last, walked into the dining room. She'd been eavesdropping around the corner. "Your mom looks like she's gonna shit," she told Sophia tactfully. "Moms aren't being like, aggressive or anything, but they're talking about gay things and about you."

Sophia sat at the table, head in her hands.

"Mom said that they won't tolerate her hurting you. That she needs to decide now if she's going to love you or not. That she doesn't get to go in and out of your life," she said, a hint of pride in her voice. "I think they said something about you living here this summer, too. Is that a thing that's happening? No one tells me anything."

Sophia looked at me, eyes wide. "I didn't know anything about that," I said. "Maybe they were just saying it was an option."

Liliana shrugged. "Maybe. They're really quiet. I tried my best to hear them but I'm sure they knew I was there." She sat down across from my girlfriend. "For the record, I'd be okay with that. You staying here, I mean. Your mom's… uh… you shouldn't have to live with that," she said, not looking up from her phone.

It was probably the nicest thing I had ever heard my baby sister say to someone who wasn't me or Cora.

"Thanks," Sophia said. "I mean, I don't know if I'm going to, but thanks." She looked shaken. "It's nice of your Moms to even offer."

I sat down next to her and pulled my chair close. She leaned forward and rested her head on my shoulder. "It's fine. This is going relatively well, I think," I told her as I rubbed her back. "Don't worry. She hasn't said anything too horrible. Mom has been good at keeping her talking. Ma has been good at shutting Mom up. We're all okay, Soph." I kissed the top of her head.

"If you guys are gonna do that all summer, I changed my mind." My sister snorted.

Sophia laughed but didn't lift her head. I raised my middle finger at Lil and kissed Sophia's head again.

"Maybe I will stay then," Sophia said. "If for no other reason but to drive you nuts." Liliana made gagging noises and Sophia laughed again, sitting up straight now.

We milled about in the dining room for the better part of a half hour, keeping fairly quiet on the off chance that we could overhear them talking in the living room. We, of course, heard nothing. Lil lingered by the doorway between the living room and the kitchen intermittently, but never came back with anything of substance. They were just talking, she said. They were just talking about Sophia and

Catholicism and lesbians. Nothing ear-catching. Nothing buzzworthy. Just talking.

I could tell Sophia was growing uneasy again.

"Dinner's ready," Cora called from the kitchen finally. Liliana jumped from the table to help her bring it in.

Moms walked in together, but Olivia wasn't behind them. Something in me went cold and I shot a nervous glance to Sophia.

"Did she leave?" There was an outside door in the living room as well as the kitchen. She could have left without even saying goodbye. She could have decided that no, she didn't want this, and taken off. Sophia's hand found my arm and slid its way to my palm. She intertwined her fingers with mine and squeezed. It wasn't until then that I realized I had no idea what answer she was hoping for. If she wanted her mother to have taken off or not.

Mom smiled. "No, she's just in the bathroom. Don't worry." She sat down on Sophia's other side. A subtle act of protection I didn't think my girlfriend—or anyone besides me—really caught. She didn't want Olivia sitting next to her. That thing inside me that froze melted with the realization that my mom really did like my girlfriend. She really did care about her.

Again, I hadn't realized I wanted her approval, too. I was so focused on Sophia getting approval from her own mother.

Mom took Sophia's free hand and squeezed her fingers briefly, before lifting her glass of water to her lips. "Your mother is…" she said after taking a sip, struggling to find a word. I wondered if the water was only a way to buy her time in that statement. "She's a lot. She has a lot of, well, work to do with all of this. But I think you two will be okay. As okay as you ever were."

I could see the tension melt out of Sophia's muscles. Her hand went lax in mine. She exhaled heavily. Had she been holding her breath?

"But I'm not sure it's in your best interest to remain living with her," Mom added. "Of course, I presume your grandmother would be more than happy to have you again. But so would we, Sophia." She smiled. "You're more than welcome to spend the summer here with us if you want."

Sophia's voice was quiet as she thanked my mother.

"No need to thank me, sweetheart. Thank *you*." Her voice was impossibly warm. "I haven't seen Annabella this happy in a long time." I felt my face flush. "I think it has a lot to do with you."

Olivia walked into the room then, face falling when she realized that Mom had claimed the seat next to Sophia. She sat across from us, between Ma and Lil. I could feel her eyes on us, but I couldn't look at anyone but Sophia. Mom's words had revitalized something in her. She looked calm and comfortable again.

I kissed her on the cheek and whispered; "You are so beautiful," against the side of her face. I didn't pull away until after I felt her smile.

"Enough with the PDA already," Lil groaned. "I swear to god, I can't live with you people."

"Maybe you were adopted," I teased.

Ma laughed. "I think we need to have a conversation about where babies come from if you girls are still uncertain on that." Even Olivia laughed at that one. She had almost the same exact laugh as Sophia. The same pink, bubbly sound that I loved. I stared across this woman who had caused my girlfriend so much pain and suffering and listened to a laugh I loved mirrored in someone I thought I should hate. This woman who bore no resemblance to the woman I cared about, who seemed to have absolutely nothing in common with her, had her laugh.

Something in me clicked.

I couldn't hate her. She gave me Sophia.

I love her. Some part of me registered the fact. It heard it, acknowledged it, felt it, but told me not to say it. I took the words and tucked them away somewhere in my lungs. Each breath was a reminder.

In: *I love her.*

Out: *I love her.*

twenty six

annabella morgan avery
summertime

Sophia did stay with me that summer. We
rushed through the rest of April and the beginning
of May in a dizzy haze of red wine and nights in
and kisses. Finals came and went and when it was
time to leave, for her to go to her grandmother's,
she told me she couldn't. That she didn't want to be
apart from me. And so she wasn't.

She told me she loved me on a Friday
afternoon in early May. We were laying in my bed
shortly after unpacking the car. I was almost asleep,
calmed by the regularity and softness of her
breathing behind me. Her arm was draped over my
torso and her face was buried in my neck.
"I love you, Annabella. I love you."

I turned my neck and kissed her. "I love you, too." It felt so good to finally say it.

Mom got her a job at a coffee shop her friend owned downtown. She was a terrible barista. I would go in every afternoon, as her shift was ending and mine at the thrift store next door was beginning. I'd order the one thing she could actually make well—tea—and wind up late for work almost every single day. I couldn't stop talking to her. I couldn't stop looking at her. Her boss always shooed us out of there a few minutes after her shift and into mine. I would kiss her outside the thrift store and my supervisor would come out, arms folded across her chest, foot tapping.

She was never really angry at me, but she liked to pretend she was. On days where Sophia didn't work and I did, she would always ask about her. Where she was, what we were doing that night, if we were happy.

The answer was always yes.

We were happy.

sophia jane kalvak

My mom came to visit on one of the first really hot days in June. My nana, who had finally reconciled with her, came too. We lounged by the pool in the Avery's backyard and Nana joked about great-grandchildren from around the world. Mom laughed, too. Real laughter.

She didn't flinch when Annabella and I touched anymore. She didn't talk about god in

hateful ways anymore. She even let me refer to god
as a woman.

When my girlfriend kissed me, my mother
looked away out of respect, not disgust.

We fought on a cold, rainy day in the middle
of the month. Holed up in Annabella's bedroom
with the door locked, even though no one else was
home. She was crying, her hands covering her face,
and my voice was barely above a whisper.
Something in me was propelling me towards her,
screaming at me for holding my ground, aching to
pull her into my arms and stop her crying.

But I couldn't.

"I love you," I was saying. "I love you,
Annabella. I love you." The words didn't feel like
love, they felt like a prison. A reminder of a
sentence I had imposed on myself. A wound that
would never heal properly.

"I love you too, you know I love you too."

"Then how can you leave me?"

We made up hours later when I crawled into
her bed sometime around midnight. I had resolved
myself to sleeping in the guest room that night to
nurse my wounds, but my skin was aching. I laid
beside her on the queen-sized mattress. The
magnets under my skin were yearning for her, but I
didn't reach out. I didn't take her hand. I kept a six
inch valley between us. I'd conceded by even
entering her bed. I needed her to go the final mile.

She stirred after a moment and I felt her
hands brush my arm beneath the covers. "Come

here," she told me. I moved closer and she took me into her arms, kissing my forehead. "I'm sorry."

No. "I'm sorry."

annabella morgan avery

In July, I kissed her underneath the fireworks. A peck for each roaring clap. Her forehead when it was green, her nose when it was blue, her cheeks when it was white, her lips when it was red. She laughed and tried to kiss me back, but I wouldn't let her spoil my game.

We spent a lot of July driving. To movies, to concerts, to beaches, to the homes of family and friends. To nowhere at all. We talked about angels and faeries and selkies and demons and god. We talked about goddesses around the world and creation myths and what happens after you die. We talked about dogs and the ethics of zoos and how sad *Blackfish* made us. It seemed like we never stopped talking.

There was nothing in the world that I didn't want to tell her about. That I didn't want to know about her. I wanted to know her opinions on everything. On morality and life and death and mythical creatures. On taxes and government and education reform. On ice cream flavors and cereal brands and air freshener scents. On my family. On her family. On herself. On me.

I felt greedy. I wanted so much. I got high off of her and her words. I never wanted to come down. I didn't think I ever would.

sophia jane kalvak

We visited Emma towards the end of July. It got so lonely up in Almost-Canada, Maine, she said. Houlton was a five-hour trek from Amherst, but Annabella was quick to agree to it. After all, Emma was my best friend.

Neither of us could get work off on the weekend, so we left early on a Wednesday morning. We almost beat the sun to the car. The thin layer of dew burned off almost as soon as the sun arrived for the day, and we cranked up the A/C as we pulled out of the driveway. Annabella was terrible at driving one handed, but she held my hand over the center console anyway.

For a while, we didn't talk. We took back roads and side streets to get to the highway and I marveled at the way Annabella could be literally by my side every single day, hand in mine in the seat next to me, and still be the sole thing on my mind. Still be the thing I couldn't stop thinking about. It was amazing to me, to not grow bored or tired of someone. To still be so in love even though we never really got a break from each other. To not *want* a break.

I caught myself praying to whatever goddesses could hear me. Frigg, Isis, Hera, Aphrodite, Sedna, Freyja. God herself.

Please let this last. Please let this survive.

I hadn't thought much about the thread Annabella said connected us, but I did then. I hoped it was made of something sturdy.

We showered together and I washed her long, thick curls for her. She pressed herself against me and kissed my nose, eyes squeezed shut. My uncertainty and worries were washed down the drain with the bubbles.

"What are you thinking about?"
"You. What are you thinking about?"
"You. Always you."

annabella morgan avery

Early August was messier.
Sophia cried a lot.
I cried a lot.
I talked myself in and out of leaving almost daily.

On the thirteenth of the month, Sophia and I went with Moms to an animal shelter. Cora's birthday was the next day and she wanted a kitten more than anything. She'd just signed a lease for an off-campus apartment that would allow her one, too.

There was a joke to be made somewhere about four lesbians looking at shelter cats, but we all seemed to be too tired to make it.

Cora had wanted a kitten. She'd been fairly clear about that. What we wound up with was a sorry excuse for a cat with a torn up ear and a missing eye. She had dry, scratchy white-and-gray fur and a smushed face. She was six years old and her name was Beauty.

We fell in love with her instantly.

"I hope Cora hates her," Mom said once we got in the car. "I hope she hates her and we get to keep her."

Ma laughed, but she couldn't disagree.

sophia jane kalvak

"How many kids do you want?"
"Two, I think."
"I think I want four."
"How about three?"
She kissed me.

Time passed strangely in August. I had lived twenty years. Been through twenty-one Augusts. This one was different. Longer but shorter at the same time. Each day felt like a lifetime, but each week was mere minutes. I was holding on to the actual hours, seconds, and minutes. Clinging to them desperately. Not realizing that it was the days and the weeks that I should have been paying attention to.

Annabella booked her flight for the 27th of August and I cried all day long.

I wasted it.

annabella morgan avery

New Hampshire started feeling less and less like home. Its mountains were beautiful but they weren't the ones I was longing for. I didn't realize I cared about mountains until then. I didn't even think I would be able to tell them apart.

I slept more, tacking on an hour to the beginning and end of the night. When I dreamed, I dreamed about Colorado.

I dreamed about Sophia come with me.

I woke up in New Hampshire with the sinking realization that she wasn't.

Would she if I asked?

"Where will we live after we finish school?"
"Wherever you want."
"I just want to be with you."
"I think we can make that happen."
She wrapped her arms around me.

sophia jane kalvak

I started waking up earlier and going to sleep later. Long after Annabella went to sleep. Long before she woke up. I averaged about four or five hours of sleep a night.

I was exhausted, always.

But I thought that the less time I spent sleeping, the more time I would have with her. The more I could make of the time I did have.

Which was foolish, of course, because she was asleep during the extra time I created. And I was mad at her for it for a while, as irrational as I knew it was. I was mad at her for not wanting more time with me. Even though I knew she did.

I didn't think heartbreak could be such a gradual process.

The day before, Annabella's Moms insisted that we all spend the day together. I almost didn't go. I almost pretended I was too sick. Almost holed myself up in her bedroom. Almost called my mom. Almost.

But Annabella wouldn't go unless I did.

So I went.

They took us out to Annabella's favorite restaurant and I cried in the bathroom. When I got back to the table, they pretended not to notice that I had been crying. Annabella held my hand under the table. We bumped knees. We played with our feet.

Orchids bloomed where she touched me.

I started crying again, worried that I wouldn't be able to keep them alive.

It was sunny the day she left. A beautiful fucking day near the end of August. I hated every bird that sang, every flower that bloomed, and every person I saw outside sunning themselves as we drove to the airport.

I tried to be angry because it was easier than being sad.

"Call me when you land." There were tears in my eyes and on my face and on my chest and probably on the floor, too. Every piece of me wanted to beg her to stay. To tell me that she changed her mind and she loved me and that I was enough. But I said nothing. I held my arms tight to my sides. I did not touch her. I did not hold her. Even though my body was aching for her.

"I will." She didn't look at me right away.

My voice cracked in two. The pieces managed to scratch out: "You promise?"

"I promise."

"I love you, Annabella."

"I love you too, Sophia."

I didn't move towards her. My body was screaming. My heart was breaking into a hundred million pieces but my legs were cemented to the floor. They called for last call boarding. She had to leave. My ribs crumbled.

"I love you, Sophia," she said again. "I love you. I love you. I love you." Still I didn't move towards her. Some part of me thought that if I didn't, she would, and she'd never turn back again.

Annabella looked over her shoulder at the disappearing line of boarders, then back at me. "Please don't make me beg, Sophia." She was crying now. "Please don't make me leave without kissing you goodbye."

"Please don't leave me." The words fell out.

"Please don't make me choose. I'm not leaving you."

"Annabella—"

"Please, Sophia. Don't make me choose. Colorado doesn't give me ultimatums." There were only five people left in line now. "Be happy for me. I'll see you at Thanksgiving. Please just be happy for me. I love you, Sophia, but if you made me choose then I don't know if I could love you anymore."

I felt cold as I closed the distance between us and kissed her. Time slowed to a standstill. Annabella pulled away from me before I was ready.

She told me she loved me. She turned around. She walked away.

She got on the plane.

annabella morgan avery

I got on the plane.

taut

sophia jane kalvak
today

Annabella was right about us being connected.
The plane took off and I felt a tugging on my finger.
I later looked up the mythology her sister told her
and found that the Chinese believed that the thread
connecting two souls didn't go through the heart,
like I'd envisioned it, but the fingers. I meant to ask
her if she felt it, too, but I never got around to it.

     The tugging went away after a while, as
most things do. They become so routine, so
commonplace, that you don't notice them anymore.
Even if they're still there. I think Annabella taught
me about that. She learned it in one of her psych
classes. If a stimuli remains unchanged, you adapt.
You make it invisible. She told me that that's why

you can't see your nose in front of your face unless you're looking for it. I'm not so sure about that, but the rest of it seemed sound.

So the stimuli remained unchanged. I didn't stop missing her. I didn't stop feeling the tugging. The stretching. The pulling. The empty space that it resulted in. But one day, I stopped noticing it so much. I couldn't see it unless I was looking right at it.

That scared me, at first. I didn't want my feelings for her to go away. I didn't want to not see them. I wanted to feel all of it, everything. I didn't want any part of it to dim. Because if my feelings dimmed, hers could, too.

But I realized that the good feelings stayed. That I was still in love with her. That she still made me happy. That the times we did see each other made me happier than I could have ever imagined I would be.

Whoever said absence makes the heart grow fonder was right. Go figure. I guess I owe them an apology.

I was projecting physicality onto this invisible, mythological thread, when it had no physical body. It could be knotted or tangled or tautened and there would be no ill effects because there was no physical string to damage. That took a while for me to get my head around. It took a while for me to understand that being connected didn't mean literally at the hip.

Our souls knew each other. That's what Nana said. Maybe they had for a long time. And one thousand nine hundred and twelve-point-two miles wasn't nearly enough to fully tauten that bond. It wasn't enough to break it.

I wasn't sure any distance would be.

I loved her. And I loved her no less in Colorado than I did in New Hampshire than I would in Tokyo than I would in Kathmandu than I would in Cape Town. I would love her in every supermarket, every ghost town, every national park, every retail outlet across the world. I would love her when I was sick, old, ugly, dying. When I was healthy, young, beautiful, alive. I loved her when she made dinner and when she forgot. When she burned out from grad school or work or law school or folding the laundry. When our kids were born and when they grew old and left us.

I loved her.

I *love* her.

Annabella, Annabella, Annabella.

Her name still tasted like spring.

Born on Cape Cod in 1995, Adrian Page has been writing since she was seven years old. When she is not writing she enjoys working with adolescents, reading up on Lesbian history and feminism. She currently lives in Massachusetts, with her wife Emily, and their furry and feathered children.